THE MISSING COUPLE

DEBRA WEBB

Recycling programs for this product may not exist in your area.

ISBN-13: 978-1-335-18906-6

The Missing Couple

For questions and comments about the quality of this book, please contact us at CustomerService@Harlequin.com.

Harlequin Enterprises ULC
22 Adelaide St. West, 41st Floor
Toronto, Ontario M5H 4E3, Canada
www.Harlequin.com

HarperCollins Publishers
Macken House, 39/40 Mayor Street Upper,
Dublin 1, D01 C9W8, Ireland
www.HarperCollins.com

Printed in Lithuania

1 2 3 4 5 6 7 8 9 10 LIT 28 27 26 25

"Billie, I...I'm..." She exhaled a big breath.

The fear in her voice had him pushing to his feet. Tension rushed through him. "What's wrong, Charly? Where are you?"

"I'm on the...end of Baker's Chapel. I need help."

"Don't hang up. I'm on my way. What happened?"

"I...was driving home from the market and a black SUV came up behind me, almost hit me, so I sped up to get away. I guess I went into the curve too fast, and I hit a pothole. The next thing I knew, I was crashed in the ditch."

A dozen knots had twisted in his gut. "Are you okay?"

"I'm okay. I think. Just shaken."

"We're going to the ER just to be sure."

No way was he going to just assume she was fine.

Not after a crash like that one.

She could have been killed.

Every instinct warned this was a direct result of their digging into his sister's disappearance.

Someone did not want them getting any closer.

Reader Note

Guntersville, Alabama, is a beautiful place. Small enough to have a tight community and yet large enough to offer tremendous fun for locals and tourists alike. Surrounded by water, Guntersville is a definite summer destination. As I always say, please know that I have the utmost confidence in law enforcement at all levels. Anything depicted in this story that might suggest otherwise is strictly fiction and for the purpose of creating tension. Also, remember that when I choose a setting, I sometimes change things to suit the story. I may completely change a street or road or the location of one or both. I sometimes add or take away things, like shops and homes. I do this primarily because I never want to use an actual home or even a street for bad things, and with a mystery or suspense story, there are bound to be bad things. I hope you'll enjoy reading this story as much as I enjoyed writing it!

Debra Webb is the award-winning, *USA TODAY* bestselling author of more than one hundred novels, including those in reader-favorite series Faces of Evil, the Colby Agency and Shades of Death. With more than four million books sold in numerous languages and countries, Debra has a love of storytelling that goes back to her childhood on a farm in Alabama. Visit Debra at debrawebb.com.

Books by Debra Webb

Harlequin Intrigue

Colby Agency: The Next Generation

A Colby Christmas Rescue
Alibi for Murder
Memory of Murder
Witness to Murder
The Husband's Secret
The Bride's Betrayal
The Missing Couple

Lookout Mountain Mysteries

Disappearance in Dread Hollow
Murder at Sunset Rock
A Place to Hide
Whispering Winds Widows
Peril in Piney Woods

Visit the Author Profile page at Harlequin.com.

CAST OF CHARACTERS

Charlotte "Charly" Nix—When a couple goes missing from her rustic retreat, she knows she must find them before it's too late.

Billie Jagger—He works for the prestigious Colby Agency, but this time it's personal—his sister is missing.

Briana and Martin Willard—Their honeymoon was supposed to be a celebration, but it turned into a nightmare.

Sheriff Tully Malone—He replaced Charly's father as sheriff after his murder. What is he hiding?

Kerrick Rogers—He was caught on the same videos with the victims. Coincidence?

Laney Rogers—She will do anything to protect her family and her business.

Paul Grant—He knows everyone in town. He's like an uncle to Charly.

Ned Bates—Five of the victims were caught on video at his convenience store.

Chapter One

Tuesday, July 7

Bradly Retreat
Deep Woods Trail
Guntersville, Alabama, 7:30 a.m.

“I am happy.”

Charly Bradly Nix stood at the window and stared out over the water from the cabin that had been home to her since she was old enough to walk. This rustic five-room structure had been home to the family—she and her sister and their parents—for the past thirty-odd years. It was small and lacking in most of the usual amenities. There was no dishwasher, no shower—just an old claw-foot tub—and no heat other than the fireplace. No air-conditioning besides the windows until two years ago.

Since she was the only one left living here now, she had considered changing the decor or maybe putting in a real shower. But honestly, she liked the place just the way it was. So much so, in fact, she had opted to keep the place even after their parents died the same year she graduated high school. Jennifer, her sister, had already met someone in college and eventually married and moved to New Jersey. She wanted no part of what she called the backwoods country life anymore. She now had three kids and a lovely old brownstone she and her husband had renovated. Every Christmas, Charly made it a point to be there for Jen and her family. It was about the only time they saw each other in person anymore.

Despite the changes with her sister and parents gone, this was the only life Charly had ever known. The only one she had wanted. With that in mind, rather than go off to college after high school, she had started the retreat. It was her parents' retirement dream, after all. Her father had planned to turn this waterfront property into a rustic vacation retreat to capitalize on the many tourists who flock to the area every year. He and her mom had often talked about spending their golden years sharing the perfect view of the still water and the silence of the woods with guests.

In the beginning, it was tough going. Charly had been basically a kid with nothing more than a little life insurance and a big plan. About five years were required to get the rustic resort out of the red financially. Ten years after that, and Charly had turned the wooded acreage that ran alongside the Tennessee River into a favored getaway for folks from all over the world. With a dozen cabins spaced far enough apart to give great privacy, she stayed booked up nearly all year round. She loved this place.

Alex had loved this place.

She blinked away the thought of her husband, Alex. "I am not lonely," she said aloud.

And she wasn't, not really. This was just a part of her morning routine, repeating her mantra aloud. Every day of the world, Charlotte "Charly" Nix got up, went for a run through the woods, showered, had breakfast and recited the words she lived by. The last part had been added after her husband's death three years ago. A friend who was also a therapist had suggested the routine.

Sometimes we just need to remind ourselves, she'd explained.

Once that ritual was behind her, Charly was ready to start her day. She sat down on the bench near the front door and tugged on her hiking boots. Last night she'd reviewed her registered guests. All but one couple had checked out yesterday as scheduled. Charly had spent Monday morning taking care of paperwork for those folks, then she'd had to make a supply run into town. By the time she'd thought of that final couple again, it had been late and she'd decided to wait until today to drop by the cabin during her usual cleaning routine.

She wasn't actually worried. Some folks left without checking in at the office, which was Charly's cabin. When that happened they generally left the key in the rented cabin. It wasn't a big deal really. She had no new guests arriving until the weekend, so she had plenty of time to get the cleaning and laundry accomplished. Still, it was nice to have the heads-up rather than being required to go check.

For now, she would carry on with her day. When she made it to cabin six, the one in question, she would ensure there were no problems and that the couple—newlyweds—hadn't decided to extend their stay. There was always the chance a miscommunication had occurred. The couple might very well have intended to stay until today. Traffic would certainly be lighter since most holiday drivers had headed home yesterday.

Setting the worry aside, Charly stepped out into the morning air. It was relatively cool for a July morning in the South. The humidity was low, which was a blessing as well as a rarity. The humidity level was one of the main reasons she wore her long brown hair in a braid all spring and summer. Otherwise, her semicurly hair would create a dark cloud around her head. Not a good look. She stepped off the porch and walked over to Lola—her aging utility terrain vehicle—and checked the supplies. Everything she needed for cleaning and restocking detail was in the good-sized toolbox she kept in the bed of the vehicle.

The cabins were spaced wide apart over the forested acreage that had been in her family for decades. Walking while carrying all the needed supplies wasn't feasible. Lola was the perfect answer. The vehicle would go pretty much anywhere. Some of the trails were rugged so four-wheel drive was a necessity.

Charly loaded up and headed out. There was a gravel road that threaded through the property with a parking area at the location of each cabin's path. Once parked, a short hike was required to reach each cabin in order to provide essential privacy and a proper nature experience. Since she had Lola, Charly could drive all the way to the cabin. The path from the parking pad to the cabin was just wide enough.

The first cabin, the Bluebird, came into view. She'd given names to all the cabins. She tried to select names that fit with the theme she'd selected for each. The Bluebird was surrounded by lovely birdhouses. Whenever Charly spotted an unusual birdhouse at one of the local shops, she added it to the collection. None were too close to the cabin to avoid the not so lovely bird droppings. But they were all visible among the trees that cloaked the cabin in privacy. Charly had commissioned rustic signs from a local artisan for each cabin, and each one was painted in a lovely color to match the design scheme she'd chosen. This first one was a pale blue with white trim.

She parked and hopped out. In truth, she couldn't take all the credit for how this retreat turned out. Alex had been the one to spearhead bringing her ideas to life. As he had so often said, she had the ideas to create the plans and he had the know-how to execute them. They'd done the work together. He'd taught her how to use all sorts of saws and other tools necessary for making and repairing things. Whether a leaky sink drain or a wonky door not closing properly, she could handle it because of all she'd learned from Alex.

They had met and married the summer she turned nineteen. A dozen years together had not been nearly long enough. A smile tugged at her lips when she considered that finally, after three years of missing him desperately, she could at least recall their time together without tears. As much as she understood that moving on was essential, she wanted to be able to remember their time together. Alex had been an amazing man and a wonderful husband. He deserved to be remembered always.

With the cabin door unlocked, Charly stepped inside. She inhaled deeply the sweet smell. Trial and error had taught her the best way to keep the cabins smelling fresh without all the fake scented sprays. Essential oils and all sorts of flowers and greenery as well as select indoor plants did the job.

Each cabin came with a kitchenette and an apartment-sized washer/dryer combo. Stuffing the linens into the washer was her first order of business. The wash cycle was generally complete by the time she finished the cleanup. She'd shift the linens to the dryer and pop the towels into the wash before moving on to the next cabin. By the end of the day she would have visited each cabin three times in total.

AS SHE ARRIVED at cabin six, the Willow, it was almost one in the afternoon and Charly's stomach reminded her that lunch should be her next stop. She decided to do a quick check of the cabin to ensure the couple had left their keys before heading back for lunch.

Although the vehicle they had arrived in was not in the designated parking spot, which suggested perhaps they had left already, Charly knocked on the door of the cabin. Walking in unannounced was not a smart move—especially considering the couple were newlyweds.

She usually tried to place newlyweds in the Willow since she considered it the perfect honeymoon cottage. The exterior was a matte white with silver and gold decor from the wind chimes to the stars and other items that adorned the exterior. A double rocker made from willow branches held center stage on the porch. Inside, plenty of willow accessories and carefully curated silver and gold pieces made the shades of white stand out.

There was no answer, even after the third knock. "Mr. and Mrs. Willard! It's Charly Nix." When there was still no answer, Charly turned the doorknob. Not locked. Another indication the couple had departed. Inside was unexpectedly cluttered.

Charly stalled and surveyed the space. The living and dining areas, including the compact kitchen, made up the front room. The smaller back room was an L shape and was comprised of a short, narrow hall that led past the bathroom and then to the bedroom. Shoehorned between the bedroom and living room was a small screened-in deck that connected the L shape to the longer front room.

Not cluttered, she realized after another slow survey of the room. *Untidy* was the better description. Clothes were on the floor. Not street clothes but sleepwear. Pajama bottoms—the new husband's, judging by the size—and a slinky nightgown.

Why on earth would they leave part of their clothes if they had left?

Had one of them gotten sick or injured and been rushed to the ER in Guntersville?

Dirty dishes sat in the sink. Not unusual. She wandered into the short hall and checked the bathroom. Toiletries were scattered about the small vanity counter. A hairbrush. Toothbrushes.

Okay. Charly stilled. This was looking more and more like the couple hadn't left yet and here she was smack in the middle of their space. Should she leave?

Well, she'd come this far. She might as well check the bedroom. The bed was unmade. When her eyes landed on the two suitcases ensconced on the luggage rack, there was no question that the couple was still here. Maybe there had been some miscommunication about the dates. The open closet door showed two summery dresses and two shirts hanging side by side. Two pairs of hiking boots sat on the floor, his and hers. Oh yeah. All their stuff appeared to still be here. As she turned to go, something else caught her eye—cell phones. She moved closer to the king-size bed. This was the only cabin with a king-size bed. All the others had either one or two queen-size beds. On the small willow tables positioned on either side of the bed were the cell phones, each plugged in for charging.

Why would the two go anywhere without taking their phones? Even a sudden need to go to the ER was generally accompanied by the urge to grab a phone along with the key fob. People who carried cell phones didn't generally like to be without them. It was a need—a comfort—to have the device handy.

Unease slid through her. Charly scanned the room more carefully now. No sign of blood or indication there had been a struggle. She checked the bathroom again, then did a slow, thorough walk-through of the front room. Nothing. No note. No blood. No indication of trouble. The nightclothes on the floor could be just a frantic urge to get naked and make love.

She decided to go back to her cabin for lunch and then check the place again. Maybe the couple would return and explain how the whole thing had been a misunderstanding. Maybe they weren't planning to leave until tomorrow.

Charly drove back to her cabin and prepared her usual lunch—a sandwich and salad. Today's sandwich was deli-sliced turkey and mayo. The salad was a mix of greens, cherry tomatoes and cucumbers with her favorite dressing. Alex had been the cook in their relationship. He would scold her for eating basically the same thing every day. She smiled before tearing off a bite of the boring sandwich. He would also fuss about the fact that she never bothered flavoring her water.

You need variety, Charly. Life is full of wonderful choices. Make a practice of selecting new ones every day.

Her smile faded when she thought of the days after that last chemo treatment when he had urged her to move on quickly. As weak as he was in his final days, he forced her to promise she wouldn't spend the rest of her life grieving and alone. She had promised she would not.

She rolled her eyes. How pathetic was it that she hadn't been able to keep her last promise to her dying husband?

Shaking off the memory, she ate her sandwich and then dove into her salad. It actually was boring. She even used the same dressing every single day. She really, really needed to start making different decisions.

"Maybe tomorrow," she muttered.

When lunch was behind her, she loaded up in Lola and headed back to the Willow. She hadn't seen the couple's vehicle return but may have missed it when she was in the bathroom.

As she arrived at her destination, her hopes fell. Still no vehicle at the parking spot. She drove to the cabin. Again, she knocked on the door. Waited. Knocked again. Waited. No response. Once more, she went inside. Everything was exactly the same.

No one had been here since she'd left an hour ago.

Charly drew in a deep breath and headed to the bedroom. She walked first to the left side of the bed and checked the phone. No notifications. She placed it back on the side table and headed around to the other side. The wife's phone, she assumed since it had a case covered with flowers, had several notifications. The final text message she had received was from a friend or coworker named Riley, who wanted to know why she wasn't answering her phone. Another was from someone named Billie, who wanted to know if she'd made it home yet.

Since there was no passcode required on the flowery-cased phone, Charly opened the calendar app and checked the dates for July. The rental dates for the cabin were indeed July third to July sixth. Lunch with Riley was on the calendar for today. Then she checked the call log. Several incoming calls last evening and today hadn't been answered, and there were no outgoing calls.

Charly placed the phone back on the table. She walked around to the husband's phone again. She touched the screen, but a passcode was required so she couldn't check his call log.

She put the phone back on the table and walked outside. She stood on the porch for a little bit and considered her next step. The dread and worry welling inside her had the urge to call the police tugging at her. Then again, she didn't want to act prematurely. Calling someone on the wife's contact list would likely upset whoever she called. But she couldn't just do nothing.

Going back into the cabin, she walked straight to the wife's side of the bed and picked up her phone. This time she disconnected it from the charger. She scrolled the contact list until she found someone listed as an emergency contact. *Billie Jagger.* Same person who sent the text message asking if she was home yet.

Charly took a deep breath and tapped the screen to make the call.

The phone rang twice and then a breathless, "Hey."

Male.

Another deep breath. "This is Charlotte Nix from the Bradly Retreat."

Silence.

"In Guntersville, Alabama," Charly added.

"Why are you using this phone?" the man asked, suspicion heavy in his tone.

She moistened her lips. "The couple who rented the Willow cabin was supposed to check out yesterday, but they didn't. I stopped by to check on them and there's no one here. All their things, including cell phones, are here, but they're gone. Their SUV is gone."

More of that silence.

Charly made a face. God, she hated to do this and be totally off base. "I'm concerned that something has happened and—"

"Why?" he cut her off. "Do you see something that makes you concerned? Signs of a struggle? Blood? Has the place been ransacked?"

She blinked, made a face. "Well…no," she admitted. "Everything looks fine. I mean, their nightclothes are on the floor, but all else appears…*normal.* Their phones were on the bedside tables, plugged in for charging. There toothbrushes are in the bathroom. I guess the part that bothers me is that none of the calls or messages they've received have been answered."

"I'm on my way."

"Hey—" The call ended before she could say more.

She stared at the screen. What the heck? She had no idea who she had just spoken to other than the man was one of the emergency contacts in the phone.

Obviously, the man—the emergency contact—felt something was wrong. Charly blew out an exasperated breath and did the only thing she could. She pulled out her own cell phone and called the sheriff's department.

If the man she'd spoken to was concerned, then she should be as well. She had been from the moment she woke up that morning…but his reaction had confirmed she was right to be.

The problem was obvious.

The couple who had rented this cabin was missing.

Chapter Two

Office
Bradly Retreat, 6:00 p.m.

The deputy in charge, Cohen Lathan, had put out a BOLO on the couple's car mostly because Charly had pushed him. They were searching the woods around Charly's property still. She wasn't so sure they would do the job the way she would, but the decision hadn't been up to her. Cohen hadn't wanted her in the way—potentially disturbing evidence and so forth.

Clearly, he wasn't aware of Charly's reputation. The guy was a couple years younger than her thirty-four years. A newbie to the area—meaning he'd only been in Marshall County for about five years. A good cop he might be, but he didn't know this place the way she did.

Exasperation swirled through her, but Charly opted not to make a fuss about his decision. She had a good relationship with the sheriff's department as well as Guntersville PD. She had no desire to step on anyone's toes. The police had their way and she had hers. When they were finished, she would redo the search using her own methods. Her father, who used to be sheriff of Marshall County, had been a fine tracker. She would bet money she knew how to follow a trail far better than the deputy leading this thing.

A forensics guy had taken fingerprints from Willow cabin and had a look around for potential evidence. All Charly could say to that was: good luck. No matter how well she cleaned, it was not possible by any stretch of the imagination that she had cleaned away all fingerprints from previous occupants. There were likely hundreds of fingerprints to be found. She rolled her eyes. Whatever. Let them look! It was their time and resources. She just wished they would wrap this up. She only had a couple of hours of daylight left, and picking through the path left by the couple and/or their abductor after the four deputies traipsed around the woods wouldn't be easy.

Charly swallowed at the tension tightening in her throat. Why would anyone abduct the honeymooners? Why here? If they were rich or had some desirable resource, had the person watching them waited until they were here—away from the security they might have back home? God. She wrapped her arms around herself. Surely, her imagination was running away with her. If someone had harmed those people…

"Don't even go there yet," she growled. No need to borrow trouble.

The two may have taken a hike and gotten lost. One could have been injured and the other was attempting to haul him or her out. Or maybe they'd made it back and gone to the ER, which would explain the missing vehicle. Except why not call or return by now? Then there was the issue of the cell phones. Certainly, the devices being left behind may have been a simple mistake. Everyone forgot their phone at one time or another.

The man from the woman's contact list, the one named Billie, hadn't called back or arrived. Depending on where he was coming from it could be tomorrow before he showed up. Then again, he may have changed his mind. But if he did call back or show up, maybe he could provide some insights into the possibilities—the ones Charly didn't want to think about.

She paced the floor some more back and forth. From her front door she could see anyone arriving up the long stretch of drive to the kitchen. The windows allowed her to see the road that disappeared deeper into her woods where the guest cabins were. The two sheriff's department cruisers were parked out front. She'd suggested the deputies use Lola for their foray deeper into her property.

Maybe they needed a helicopter. A rescue team.

Finally, the distant sound of Lola's engine brushed her ears. Charly hurried outside. Her heart rate climbed a dozen more beats per minute as she watched her UTV roll into view. As soon as the vehicle stopped and the engine shut down, four lanky deputies climbed out. The grim set to their expressions warned they hadn't found anything.

Cohen swaggered up to her. "Well, Ms. Nix, we didn't find a sign of anyone or any indications of foul play. Once a missing persons report is filed we can start an *official* search." He adjusted his sunglasses. "Fact is it would be very helpful if you could reach a relative who knows about this couple. We need as much information as we can get about where they may have gone or what kind of trouble they might have been in. The whole honeymoon thing could have been a cover."

Charly would really like to argue the idea, but the

truth was she couldn't say. The two seemed nice. She'd had no reason to suspect they were anything more than what they presented themselves to be. As much as she wanted to protect her guests, she couldn't prove anything one way or the other.

"I appreciate the effort," she assured him. "You'll let me know if you hear anything back on that BOLO or those fingerprints?" The last she said just to be nice. She had zero hopes that effort would be useful in any way.

A new worry had started to gnaw at the edges of her mind.

What if the two actually had been abducted? What if they had come here as an escape from some sort of trouble? Charly considered the fact that the reservation had been made weeks ago so that really didn't seem feasible. Then again, they may have been planning whatever had gotten them into trouble for months.

The whole idea sounded ludicrous.

The sound of another vehicle arriving drew their collective attention toward the road that wound through the acres and acres of woods that separated the retreat from the main highway. SUV. Black. Too shiny to be from around here. Even as the thought occurred to her, dust from the gravel drive that the vehicle's movement had stirred up began to settle on its glossy exterior.

"You expecting another guest?" Lathan asked.

"No. Not until Friday." Charly studied the tinted windows. She couldn't tell yet if there was one person in the vehicle or more…man or woman.

"Maybe your missing couple got a new ride," another deputy suggested with a half-hearted chuckle.

"Maybe," Charly agreed rather than tell him that

wasn't very likely. But then again, maybe she was wrong. Wouldn't be the first time. Maybe their rental broke down and they got another one.

The SUV found a spot away from the two cruisers and parked. The driver's-side door opened and Charly couldn't help holding her breath.

Male. Blond hair.

Not Martin Willard—the groom who'd brought his bride here for a quick honeymoon. Martin had black hair. His new wife, Briana, had blond hair.

The man who'd emerged from the SUV wore all black, shirt, trousers and a lightweight jacket. Even his shoes were black. She would bet his socks and underwear were as well.

"That's not one of the missing guests," Charly said, putting all the uniforms at ease.

The blond-haired man's gaze scanned the group before narrowing in on her. "Are you Charlotte Nix?"

Charly descended the two steps off her porch. "I am."

"I'm Billie Jagger. You called me."

She nodded. "You sent that text message to Mrs. Willard."

He surveyed the deputies once more. "Is there an update? Has Briana returned?"

"I'm afraid—" Charly began but Deputy Lathan cut her off with, "Let's see some ID, sir." He stepped closer to the new arrival.

Billie Jagger didn't hesitate. He removed his wallet from his hip pocket and showed his driver's license.

"Chicago," Lathan said. He harrumphed. "How do you know Mr. and Mrs. Willard?"

"Briana is my sister."

"Have you heard from your sister in the last twenty-four hours?" Lathan asked while one of the other deputies walked around the man's SUV as if he suspected he was hauling contraband.

"I have not," Billie said. "When I last saw her or spoke to her she was in a limousine heading to the airport with her new husband. They were supposed to be back in Chicago yesterday afternoon."

"Do you know of any reason one or both might want to disappear?" Lathan went on.

Charly hadn't gotten the impression from the newlyweds that either of them wanted anything but each other. What was Lathan implying? Was there something he hadn't told her? She'd briefly toyed with the idea after he brought it up, but he spoke now as if he knew something. Maybe only to prompt a particular reaction from this man.

Billie shook his head. "None at all. If my sister and her husband are missing, something has happened to them. They wouldn't do this sort of thing willingly."

Lathan's gaze narrowed with suspicion. "What sort of thing?"

Dear God. What was he doing? This man's sister was missing!

"Deputy—" Billie looked to the name tag on the other man's shirt "—Lathan, I'm aware you don't know my sister and her husband. I understand you have to look at any disappearance from all angles. But I really wish you wouldn't waste precious time. If my sister is not where she said she would be, then something has happened to her. End of story."

Well, the stranger sure told Cohen with that one.

Charly pressed her lips together to prevent a smile. "You call me," she said to the deputy, "the instant you get something back on the vehicle."

Cohen glanced at Charly, clearly annoyed by her attempt at a dismissal, then turned back to Billie Jagger. "I'll need your number. I'm sure we'll have more questions."

Billie reached into his jacket, retrieved what appeared to be a business card and handed it to the deputy. "I'll have questions as well—once we've had time to figure out what's going on here."

"You come to the office tomorrow and file a missing persons report," Lathan directed. "Assuming the couple doesn't show up by then." He hitched his head toward the cruisers and the four swaggered away.

Admittedly, Charly had never known the department to do anything except its best. Lathan was just cocky. Trying to show out for her and anyone else who might be looking. Some guys were like that.

"I have questions for you."

The sound of Billie Jagger's voice drew her attention back to him. "Sure." Charly gestured to her cabin. "Come on in and I'll tell you everything I know."

She stepped onto the porch and walked across it, left the door open for him to follow her inside. He closed it behind him and she took the opportunity to size him up a little better. Six feet at least. Broad shouldered. His hair was cut shorter in front but brushed his collar in the back. Blue eyes, she was pretty sure. When his gaze landed back on her, he gave her the same treatment—a thorough perusal. Yep, blue eyes. She wore a vintage gray Bradly Retreat tee and equally vintage—

aka worn—jeans. Nothing fancy. Charly had never been a fancy person.

"Can you walk me through your interactions with the Willards from the time the reservation was made until you noticed they were missing?" He moved a step or two closer. "Specific details, please. Dates, times, method of communication. Those sorts of particulars."

She nodded. "Sure. You want to sit?" She gestured to the sofa.

He walked around to the other side of the sofa but didn't sit until she did. Charly took the chair she considered hers—the one her husband had loved—and waited until her visitor had settled on the sofa. "Briana made the reservation online six weeks ago. A week ago, Friday before last, before their arrival, she called and confirmed all was set."

He waited through her pause. Said nothing. Only stared at her.

"On Friday, July third, they arrived at about three in the afternoon. They were driving a white Ford SUV. A rental from an agency at the Huntsville airport. Both were literally beaming." She smiled at the memory of the happy couple. "It was obvious they were madly in love and excited for this getaway."

He slipped his cell phone from a jacket pocket and searched for something before getting up and walking over to where she sat. "Was this the couple who checked in?"

The question startled Charly but then again, she supposed it was a good one to ask. Obviously, she had been provided with the husband's driver's license when he arrived, but she supposed it could have been a fake. She studied the photo on his phone. Briana and Martin were smiling widely, still sporting their wedding attire.

"Yes. That's them."

Billie put his phone away and resumed his seat. "Did you see or speak with either of them after they checked in?"

Charly replayed the weekend, then yesterday. Taking her time as she sifted through the memories. "No. As far as I am aware they never left the cabin once they arrived."

He digested this information. "Are there delivery services available? Like DoorDash?"

"Yes." She nodded. "A couple, in fact. DoorDash and Uber Eats. Some restaurants have their own delivery as well."

"Do you know if they used any of those services?"

Charly wished she'd had cameras put in ages ago, but she and Alex had worried that their guests wouldn't like the intrusion. "I can't say one way or the other. I don't have cameras here and I'm not always where I can see comings and goings."

Another lengthy pause. "When the deputies were in the cabin, did they take the trash?"

"I can't be sure. They sent me back here." Charly frowned. "But when they returned they had nothing with them. The forensics guy stopped by on his way out, and he didn't mention taking anything. And I didn't see anything."

"The trash might tell us if they had food delivered."

Charly nodded. She should have thought of that. "You're right. We could go have a look."

He stood. "I would appreciate that."

Charly grabbed her keys. "We'll take Lola."

He didn't ask but she saw the question on his face. She smiled to herself. He'd know the answer soon enough. She climbed into the UTV and waited while he did the same on the passenger side. Lola didn't have doors but that was okay with Charly. Made getting in and out much easier.

She drove to the parking area, which she pointed out to him, and then on to the Willow. The sun had set, and it would be dark soon. Too late to search tonight but she would start first thing in the morning. As Cohen had explained, unless there were obvious indications of foul play or extenuating circumstances like a vulnerable adult, missing persons reports would have to wait a full twenty-four hours, which was stupid in Charly's opinion. But at least there was a family member here to provide incentive.

She walked to the door and unlocked it, but Billie didn't follow. Instead, he walked around the corner of the cabin. Charly shrugged and followed his path. He checked each window he encountered. Inspected the patio door on the screened deck. Then checked the remaining windows as he made his way back around front. As he walked, he carefully surveyed the ground. She supposed he was looking for areas of trampled grass and wildflowers where someone might have stared through a window.

Once they were inside, she waited while he took a tour of the cabin. He thoroughly examined every cabinet, drawer, nook and cranny. The small trash can beneath the sink revealed a bag delivered by a DoorDash driver. He removed the sales receipt that was still attached, looked over it and then tucked it into his pocket.

"They received a food delivery on Saturday night."

Charly nodded. It was a starting place at least. That one piece of paper suggested they had been in the cabin on Saturday night.

Billie conducted the same thorough perusal of each room. He sniffed their shampoo. The soap and the toothpaste. She might have been startled but she'd read enough mystery novels to understand he was looking for some sort of poison or sedative that may have been added to their products. The idea that he knew what he was doing a little too well crossed her mind. Was he a cop? A private investigator?

Seemed reasonable.

When he finally appeared to be satisfied he'd seen everything, she asked, "What do you think?"

"I think I need to stay here until I find my sister and her husband."

Charly nodded. "Of course. I'm sure you're very worried." Actually, it was difficult to say. He seemed intent. Focused. He'd shown few other emotions. She was extremely worried herself.

"I would like the cabin closest to this one if it's available."

Oh, so he literally meant he wanted to stay *here*. "Of course. Sure. The other guests all checked out yesterday. I haven't cleaned number seven but number five, the Treehouse, is ready."

"Treehouse?" His expression told her he wasn't sure what she meant.

"It's exactly what it sounds like." Cabin five had been

Alex's baby. A treehouse. He'd seen an article on the topic in some magazine and decided they had to have one. "It's a cabin but it's suspended between two massive trees. The stairs up to it wind around one of the trees. It's quite unique and gives you a bit of a view from above."

"Sounds perfect."

"I'll take you back to your SUV and get the key from the office."

As they drove back, she pointed out the parking spot for the Treehouse. Of course there was a sign but it was getting darker. Better to be sure he had a grasp on the location.

At the office while he waited, oddly patiently, she put together a basket. She was sure he hadn't brought anything with him for this sort of situation, so she packed bottled water and a couple of sodas as well as chips and other snacks. Luckily, she had a few power bars. For good measure she tossed in a couple of candy bars. The wicked sugary, chocolatey kind.

When she felt she had put together a decent offering, she thrust the basket at him. "I figured you weren't prepared for this sort of lodging."

He accepted the basket. "Thanks."

She followed him onto the porch. She'd been right. It was mostly dark now. A big moon and blanket of stars provided some amount of light. There was little artificial lighting around the retreat.

She had to know one thing before they parted ways for the night. "Billie."

At the bottom of the steps, he paused and turned back to her.

"It is possible they just took off for an unexpected excursion and left a message for me at the wrong number." She shrugged. "Maybe they're coming back tomorrow."

His somber gaze was answer enough even before he spoke. "Doubtful."

Fifteen years she had been running this place. From the days of renting out spots for tents and small campers to the build of each of the cottages. Not once—ever, ever, ever—had a guest been injured or robbed or bothered in any way.

She sure as hell had never lost one.

"You—" she shrugged again "—believe we need to be worried, I mean really worried, about them."

"Yes."

And then he was gone.

Chapter Three

Wednesday, July 8

Treehouse
Bradly Retreat, 7:45 a.m.

Billie had been awake for hours. At seven he'd called the sheriff's office and made sure the official missing persons reports were filed for Briana and Martin. To his surprise, the sheriff had insisted on taking care of the matter personally. A news conference was scheduled at noon.

After that, Billie had tried to focus on how to move forward. He'd attempted to relax. To focus on anything but the facts for a moment. With that in mind, coffee in hand, he leaned against the deck railing and stared into the woods. The trees were too thick and too heavily canopied to see very far. The sounds of the forest were subtle…almost soothing.

Except his sister and her new husband were missing.

To hell with relaxing. He forked his fingers through his hair. How the hell had this happened? There was no indication of anyone from his past having initiated some sort of payback. He'd had his resources at the Colby Agency search not only his past cases but also any potential issues in the area of Guntersville. So far, they had nothing, even though it had been about eighteen hours since he learned Briana was missing.

He shook his head. This was off. Way off. If she'd been kidnapped, why had there been no ransom demand by now? If she and Martin had decided to take an off-the-itinerary excursion, why not find a phone and let someone know? That sort of reckless behavior was not his sister's style. She was meticulous about everything. Her schedule. Her home. A laugh choked out of him. Her hair. She was six years younger than Billie's thirty-five, but she'd been born an organizer. Which made her perfect for forensic accounting. No one was better. More important, she had a kind heart.

A smile tugged at his lips. She had to be okay…

He pushed away from the railing and walked back into the cabin—treehouse. He had to hand it to whoever designed the small space; it was very well thought out. There were shelves and drawers in every potential spot. The beds were built into the wall, giving the exterior a completely "un-rectangular" feel. The structure was all curves with minimal true angles, none of which were standard fare. It was almost wonky. But in a very cool way.

Billie couldn't remember the last time he'd taken a vacation. He was too focused on work. Gaining a spot at the Colby Agency had been his dream for several years. When Jamie Colby, the granddaughter of matriarch Victoria, had called him with the news two years ago, he'd been stoked. He had barely taken a day off…until now.

He left his cup in the small, round kitchen sink and went in search of a suitable shirt. He'd been at work when he received that call yesterday. He'd taken just enough time to throw a few things into a bag and then his boss, Victoria, had kindly offered the agency jet for rushing him down to Alabama. Jamie had arranged for a rental car to be waiting for him at the Guntersville Municipal Airport.

The next best step, he decided as he buttoned the shirt, was to have a look around the cabin where Briana and Martin had stayed. If the BOLO issued by the police turned up something on the rental SUV first, that would be great. For now, he intended to start at ground zero and work his way outward.

He stepped out onto the front deck just in time to spot the retreat owner buzzing up the path in her UTV. She braked to a stop and hopped out. Her brown hair was pulled into a long braid. Like yesterday, she wore a tee and jeans with her hiking boots. Today's jeans were different. They were the more utilitarian-cargo type with extra pockets on the legs, all of which looked to be stuffed with something. At least two held water bottles. He descended the steps, winding around the trunk of the tree until he was face-to-face with her on the ground.

"Morning," she said with a nod. "You sleep okay?"

"Not that great," he admitted, studying her green eyes. She had really dark green eyes. "Worrying about someone you love will do that."

The hopeful look in her eyes faded to something unreadable. "Yeah. You're right." She gestured toward the trail. "I was about to head over to the Willow and start looking around. I thought you might want to join me."

"I was just about to head that way myself." He imagined finding two missing guests was important to her as well. If they weren't found, it wouldn't look good for her business.

"You had breakfast?" she asked as they walked toward her ride.

"One of those protein bars and coffee. Does that count down here in the South?"

"Close enough in my opinion." She slid behind the wheel. "Every breakfast doesn't have to include grits and biscuits."

He laughed in spite of the worry twisting in his gut. "I guess you're right."

The ride to the Willow took only a few minutes. No cops around. He wished he could have gotten a look at the scene before the locals, but there was no help for that. They exited the UTV and Charly walked straight to the cabin and unlocked the door.

"We could have a look inside again," she offered, "but personally, I'd like to start in the woods."

"Lead the way." He didn't mention this was his preference as well. He was surprised she would have the same thought. Maybe she didn't put too much stock in the deputies' work yesterday, either.

Billie had no reason to feel that way but there had been a sort of nonchalance about the deputies he'd met last evening. This was Billie's sister. There was nothing nonchalant about the situation.

As Billie had done late yesterday, Charly walked all the way around the house, scanning the ground, shrubs and bushes. The second go-around, she stopped at the steps from the deck and stared into the woods. He wondered if she had spotted something.

He hung back and scrutinized the area she'd taken

the longest to analyze. A smile stretched across his face. Right there at the corner of the bottom step was the tiniest snag in the dirt as if a heel had gotten caught in it. He straightened and headed in the direction Charly had gone.

She picked her way through the woods, surveying the ground and everything around her. Trees, shrubs… wild grasses, scattered flowers and weeds. From time to time she stopped and inspected something more closely.

The next time she stopped, he moved in close behind her. "What are you seeing here?"

"Heel marks." She glanced up at him then pointed to the small, shallow indentation in the ground. "Your sister's hiking boots are still in the closet so I'm guessing she left the cabin in whatever shoes she arrived in. What was she wearing when she left for the airport?"

"A white—kind of off-white, like a pearl actually—formfitting dress." His brow furrowed as he called the image to mind. "Dress hit around the tops of her knees. High-heeled shoes that matched the dress."

"What kind of heels? Pointy? Platform? Wedge?"

He held his forefinger and thumb about three inches apart. "The skinny, pointy ones about this long. Those are her favorite. I doubt she would have left home without at least two pairs."

Charly pointed to the indentation. "That's a pointy heel impression."

His smile tried to reappear. "You're very good at this." He would have done exactly as she had, but watching her had been far more…interesting. And, he had to admit, she appeared to be better than him at the business of tracking.

"This—" she pointed to an area of flattened greenery on the ground "—is a deputy's footprint. Notice the vague waffle-like grid. The boots they were wearing have that pattern. This print was going back to the cabin so we've already gone as far as they did when they looked yesterday."

Oh yeah. She was good.

"Lead on," he suggested.

She started moving again, her gaze roving the ground and then the area around her in a constant close pattern. Every hesitation had his neck prickling. He knew little about the area. Basically nothing, actually. But this wasn't his first hike in the woods and based on his drive from town, these wooded acres were nestled between the road and the river. The aerial view he'd found while searching for info during the flight showed a thickly wooded property. If his memory was correct, they were moving away from the river and toward the road that ran the length of the property.

The trail had started at the cabin and through the woods to the north before heading east toward the road.

BY TEN, THEY HAD covered a considerable distance, and the sun was higher in the sky, beating down on them wherever the tree canopy parted. The air was heating up. So far, nothing more than the same types of indications that his sister had come this way had been found. The ground was drier in this direction, the incline higher. Other than the occasional indentation made by Briana's heels and the sporadic broken limb on a bush, there wasn't a lot to go on, but Charly didn't miss any disruption in the landscape. He was seriously impressed at this point.

He bumped into her back.

An *oomph* issued from his throat. “Sorry. I should have been watching more carefully.”

She stared forward. He stepped up next to her since the space between the two trees where she stood allowed for it. He looked from her to where she stared.

“Listen,” she whispered as if someone might be nearby and she didn’t want them to hear what she had to say.

He did as she said and listened intently. A moment passed before he heard anything beyond the birds and rustling of the leaves they’d been hearing for a couple of hours. “Is that an engine? A car or truck?” he asked.

“Yeah. We’re really close to the road.” She stared at the ground. “It’s obvious they were brought this way for that purpose. If I had my guess, the trouble came to the cabin from this direction as well. Either way, whoever was with them knew the kind of footwear that wouldn’t leave a recognizable imprint.” She crouched down. “See that impression?”

He crouched next to her. “I do.” It was nothing more than a slightly flattened grass area—didn’t penetrate the ground’s surface. Too dry here “We’ve seen a few of those, some with a tad more depth. You’re sure all four deputies were wearing the same grid pattern-soled boots?”

She nodded. “Positive. It’s the department’s issued footwear.”

“Then the question is,” Billie said, “why was their vehicle taken off the property while they were brought this way?”

“Easy.” She pushed to her feet. “If anyone happened to be walking around the retreat and saw anything that night, it would appear they had driven away. If the vehicle was seen rolling through town it would, again, give the impression they had left of their own volition."

Billie laughed. "If I didn't know better I'd say you were an investigator in a former life." He knew she'd only ever been the owner of this retreat other than her short waitressing stint during high school. Charly Nix was another bit of research he'd done on the flight from Chicago to Guntersville.

"My father taught me to pay attention." She shrugged. "He used to be the sheriff in Marshall County. And a hunter. He said when push comes to shove, your best defense is in the details. Every little detail matters."

"Smart man." He glanced at the ground again. "You ready to keep going?"

"Ready." She started forward once more.

They discovered the same evidence for the next few minutes as they'd found when they started—right at that step coming down from the deck at the cabin. Eventually, the forest gave way to a grassy right-of-way on the roadside. The highway cut through right in front of them. Traffic appeared to be sparse.

Charly did her magic. Studying the ground until she found what she was looking for. She squatted down a few feet from the pavement and looked closer.

"Another heel impression here. Then this line of smashed grass. It's springing back up now, but it was flattened for a bit."

"A vehicle pulled to the side of the road here," he said.

"Yep. Could have been any vehicle passing through except for that heel indentation." She stood. "This is where they got into a vehicle and drove away."

Billie studied the grass and weeds. It had been cut in

recent weeks so it wasn't that tall, but it was clear to see the vehicle had left going north. He scanned the road in both directions as far as he could see. No CCTV of any sort out in the country like this.

He turned back to Charly. "We should go back and get my SUV. I'd like to follow the road. Maybe someone who lives in one direction or the other has a video doorbell."

Charly didn't look optimistic. "There are houses. Not that many. Some likely too far from the road to help even if they have a camera doorbell."

He nodded an acknowledgment. "All it takes is one."

"Right," she admitted.

They started back through the woods. His cell vibrated in his pocket. He withdrew it, recognized the local area code. He answered with "Jagger."

"Mr. Jagger, this is Deputy Lathan. We met yesterday."

"Yes, Deputy Lathan." Billie glanced at Charly. They both stopped as if being still was necessary for hearing whatever the man had to say. Fear raced down Billie's sternum and lodged in his heart.

"We found your sister's rental."

The fear expanded. "Anything inside?" What he wanted to ask was whether she was inside but that terror currently choking him wouldn't allow it.

"No bodies. Nothing relevant other than a handbag with your sister's ID and such in it."

Billie felt some measure of relief at hearing no bodies were found—at least not yet. "Where did you find it?"

"In the water off Sunset Drive," Lathan said. "Whoever disposed of it here underestimated the tenacity of the local treasure hunters. Ever since that docuseries about finding lost gold coins and treasure, someone's always poking around with that magnet fishing stuff."

"I'd like to see the vehicle."

Lathan gave him the location of the county's property and evidence compound and said he'd be waiting.

Billie ended the call. "They found the vehicle she and Martin rented. It was in the water."

"Is it at the evidence shed?"

Billie nodded.

"Come on." She hurried forward once more. "I know the place. I used to play there as a kid."

Billie followed. He wanted to be relieved there was no body…but he wasn't. As much as this was a good thing, it was also a very bad thing.

Someone had taken his sister, and likely her husband as well, by force, but they weren't reaching out for a ransom or whatever it was they were after.

The options outside a ransom of some sort were not ones he wanted to consider but at this point he had no choice.

His sister's life depended on him and on the lady keeping pace with his wide strides.

He'd never really liked the idea of a partner. He preferred working alone. But he had a feeling he was going to need this woman.

Chapter Four

Marshall County Evidence Shed
Worth Street, 11:50 a.m.

When her father was sheriff—forever ago—Charly had loved coming here to play. The rules were a little different then. She doubted the current sheriff would bring his kids here. But Charly hadn't been the usual kid. She'd loved to read—mysteries of course—and she'd loved trailing along after her father. Whether he was hunting or reviewing evidence, he was her idol. Some girls her age had been enthralled with movie stars or whoever was at the top of the music charts, but not Charly.

The white Ford SUV had been towed to the shed, arriving just ten or so minutes before she and Billie. Sheriff Tully Malone was on the way over. He, apparently, had decided to hold the press conference early. Charly suspected the change in timing was about keeping Billie away from the press.

Billie wasn't happy about it but kept his cool. Even when the sheriff arrived, he made no fuss about being left out. Sheriff Malone had obviously concluded that such an official high-level crime needed his personal involvement and any and all credit should be his—however this ended. Except, she mused, if it didn't go well then he'd likely find someone else to give credit. Charly chastised herself for thinking such a thing. Tully Malone was a good sheriff. He'd been on the job since her father died—sixteen years.

Died. Charly had learned to look at what happened to her parents that way because it did no good to anyone, especially her, to be reminded that her father and her mother had been murdered by a cold-blooded killer. One who had shot and killed them and just walked away. Her parents had been on the way home together that night. No doubt she and Jen would have been murdered, too, if they'd been with them. But Jen was already off at college and Charly had gone to Birmingham to visit her. Charly was just weeks away from high school graduation and was slated to attend the same university.

But everything changed after that night.

Charly snapped from the memory as the sheriff's deep voice filtered through the haze of the past.

"Our people will go over the vehicle carefully," Malone was saying. "We'll keep you advised of any details we find."

Charly looked from Sheriff Malone to Billie. She was surprised that the sheriff had chosen to be so forthcoming about an investigation that was obviously not just about a stolen vehicle. It certainly wouldn't be because he considered Charly a good friend. Although she couldn't deny that he seemed to be a decent sheriff, there remained a thread of tension between them. Mostly due to her behavior after the murders of her parents.

She had been in shock, clearly. But in her earlier years

she had followed her father around and hung on his every word enough to know the whole thing didn't feel right. Why couldn't a single shred of evidence be found? Why was the killer never discovered? It was as if the whole thing never happened. The murders of her parents remained unsolved to this day. No rumors. No nothing.

Once more, she kicked the past back to its place. Just in time to notice Billie and the sheriff shaking hands.

"We will keep you informed," Sheriff Malone assured him. "We'll give you a look at the handbag as soon as our people have had time to process it. If our hotline turns up anything, you'll be the first to know."

"I appreciate that, Sheriff," Billie said.

"The head of your agency called," the sheriff explained. "I assured her that my department would provide any additional support you need. We all want the same thing here—to find your sister and her husband."

Surprise registered and Charly resisted the impulse to ask what the sheriff meant. It was better to wait and ask Billie when they were out of here.

Billie thanked him again and turned to Charly. Since she had nothing to add that concerned the sheriff, they headed for the exit.

She glanced at the white SUV sequestered to one of the three bays in the shed. They hadn't been allowed to look inside or even get close but there was nothing to see. Prints and most other potential evidence would be long gone considering the windows had been opened before sending the vehicle into the murky water.

Once she and Billie were back in his high-end black SUV, she turned in the passenger seat to study his profile. "What did Sheriff Malone mean when he said the head of your *agency*?"

Wouldn't be the FBI; it was a bureau. Wouldn't be DEA; that was an administration.

He hesitated before starting the engine. He turned to her. "I'm a private investigator. I work with the Colby Agency. But that's not why I'm here. I'm here because my sister and her husband are missing. If the identity of my employer provides some amount of leverage toward that end, I'm grateful."

Charly nodded. "I see." Now she felt like a total idiot for taking the lead in those woods when a real, honest-to-God, probably highly trained, PI had been right next to her.

He started the engine and pulled out onto the street.

"I guess your boss is pretty important to have captured Sheriff Malone's attention with a single phone call."

Billie glanced at her as he navigated traffic. "She's not your average boss."

Charly pulled out her phone and started to google this Colby Agency. She felt his eyes in her direction a couple of times but that didn't deter her. Line after line of results filled the screen. She started with the top hit. The more she read the more startled she became. He was not kidding when he said his boss wasn't the average sort. Neither was the agency.

She stared at him, and he glanced her way. "Told you," he said with a slight smile.

"Your agency is no run-of-the-mill private investigations firm," she said before she could stop herself. "Your boss..." Charly wasn't even sure how to frame what she'd just read about Victoria Colby-Camp. The woman was known all over the world. "She's an icon, it seems."

"I'm very fortunate," he said, sending another look her way, "to be a part of the Colby Agency. But I'm on leave and this investigation is personal."

Charly reminded herself to close her mouth, which had been gaping since she started reading the results from her search.

Apparently taking her silence as a need for further explanation, he went on. "I didn't mention my work because I didn't want you to feel you couldn't speak freely or do what you normally do around me here."

Might be a little late for that. But she got it. His sister was missing, and he didn't want to make this about him.

"FYI," she explained, "I have never felt the need to suppress whatever I had to say when it was relevant. No need to worry about me."

He gave her a nod. "Good."

She thought about what to pass along next. Sometimes it was extra important to weigh words before they were spoken. Not exactly her best quality.

"Seems the sheriff is taking the situation seriously. I mean, it's obvious Briana and Martin were taken by force. But I would have liked to hear more about his strategy."

"Agreed." He made the turn onto Blount Avenue. "The usual protocol once a kidnapping is confirmed is to call in the FBI."

"But usually with a kidnapping—if it's not personal—it's for some sort of ransom, right?" she tossed out. It was reasonable to see kidnapping at the top of the list of potential causes for the couple missing. The motive behind the move remained a mystery in this case.

"Yes." He exhaled a big breath. "But I haven't received a call or text to suggest there's a ransom request, which is troubling. Generally, that would have happened by now."

"This would be a pretty stupid kidnapper if he didn't know who the target he intended to exploit was before taking anyone as collateral." A new thread of uneasiness stitched its way through Charly. "Unless this is more about what the victims offer."

Of course it was possible the kidnapping was some random event related to wrong place/wrong time, but the scene was far too clean for an unplanned event. This felt more like an experienced kidnapper who knew what he was after before selecting the target.

Billie slowed again, this time to turn onto Taylor Street. "If this was a spur-of-the-moment grab," he said as he parked at her cabin, "then their bodies would have been in that SUV."

His words sent a chill through her. "That's it, then. You're worried it's not a ransom situation, not a random act of violence, but something related directly to Briana and Martin."

Like their value as a marketable commodity, she didn't say out loud. The idea made her sick.

"Human trafficking is real—even in small communities with low crime rates," he explained. "You get a lot of tourists—with that kind of influx there's bound to be trouble once in a while. Then there's the possibility of revenge against me or my sister or her husband." Another look arrowed Charly's way. "Or maybe you. Finding the something that triggered this event—the motive—will take time, and time is our enemy."

She got the point but… "I hope I have never done anything that would prompt this kind of act."

"Just saying," he offered, "there are lots of reasons people go missing. Sometimes the cause is the last thing we expect."

She nodded, then frowned as she surveyed the street they'd turned onto. Where were they going? She started to ask but then he pulled into the short driveway at a little white house located only a short distance before Taylor turned into Albert Smith Drive. She had obviously missed something.

He shut off the engine. "I have a resource at the agency who will be sending me a complete list of where and when their credit and debit cards were used since leaving Chicago." He set his full attention on Charly. "Until I get that list I need to be doing what I can. This is the home of the delivery guy, Teddy Sowell, who dropped off the food bag we found in the trash at the cabin. You want to go in with me? Having someone local with me could go a long way on gaining trust."

"Definitely." She wasn't sure how he'd gotten the information, but she was glad he had. She scanned the place as she reached for her door. A privacy fence shrouded the backyard. Parked next to the house was a compact car. Hopefully, that meant someone was home.

They met at the front of his SUV. "I'm operating on the assumption that Briana and Martin will have encountered the perp somewhere here after their arrival."

Made sense. "I wish I could be more helpful about their comings and goings," Charly offered, "but the truth is they could have gone anywhere at any time without me noticing."

She was getting cameras even if only at the entrance to her retreat. It was the single way in or out of the property via anything other than a utility vehicle or on foot.

A little late for Briana and Martin.

Charly pushed aside the depressing thought and walked alongside Billie to the front door. The first thing she heard was a deep, threatening series of barks. Beyond that, and at a somewhat lower volume, was the chatter of a television. Billie knocked and the television volume lowered while the barking grew louder.

Definitely someone home.

The wood door opened and a middle-aged man wearing nothing but gym shorts peered through the screen door. "I have my own religion and I don't need your pamphlets."

"Mr. Sowell, my name is Billie Jagger. I'm looking into a case involving a couple who was staying at the Bradly Retreat."

The man glanced at Charly and his expression shifted as if he recognized her on some level.

"Yeah? What's that got to do with me?" The raucous barking started again. "Hang on a minute." He disappeared into the house. The sound of him scolding his dog and ordering him into the backyard drifted to where they waited at the front door.

When he returned to the door, confusion and distrust lined his face. "What's this about?"

"You made a delivery from a local restaurant to the Willow Cabin on Saturday night at around seven-thirty."

The man's gaze narrowed in on Billie. "Who told you that?"

"Mr. Sowell..." Charly stepped forward, nearly pressing her face into the screen mesh that separated them. "We're not here about your work. This isn't about you. We're here to ask you about what you saw and anything the couple staying at the Willow said while you were there."

The man was clearly suspicious of their abrupt appearance at his door and didn't feel comfortable being questioned about his work. Charly got it. There were folks around here who didn't like anyone nosing into their business. Billie might not understand that considering he was from such a large city.

Mr. Sowell scrubbed a hand across his chest. "Let me get a shirt on and y'all can come in." He wandered back into the house once more.

"Thanks," Billie said quietly.

She looked up at the man next to her. "He just needed reassuring that we weren't looking into his personal business."

Billie lowered his chin in acknowledgment of her explanation.

Mr. Sowell appeared at the door again. "Come on in."

Billie opened the screen door and waited while Charly walked inside ahead of him. The place was dimly lit, more than a little cluttered and smelled a bit on the stuffy side. The furnishings gave her the impression of an older woman's touch. Maybe he inherited the place from his mom or maybe she lived here, too.

"Sorry about the mess," he apologized. "I worked

eighteen hours a day for the last three and I'm beat. My mother's disabled and can't do much anymore."

"I imagine all the deliveries keep you pretty busy," Charly said. Delivery was immensely popular these days. She didn't eat out much, so she hadn't used the service in ages.

Mr. Sowell plopped into a well-worn recliner. "I work maintenance at the hospital in the daytime and then deliver at night. You wouldn't believe it. There are some people who never go out anymore and the rest only do on special occasions. I swear, everyone stays home now."

"It's the same way in the big city," Billie chimed in.

Mr. Sowell eyed him a little suspiciously, even now. "So what's the deal with this couple?"

Charly kept quiet. She figured it was better to let Billie reveal whatever he thought needed to be told.

"My sister, Briana, and her new husband, Martin." Billie smiled. "They came here for a short honeymoon and now they're missing."

Mr. Sowell pulled a confused face. "Missing? Like in vanished?"

"Everything they brought to that cabin is still there—except the two of them," Billie confirmed. "The police are investigating the case."

"Wow." He ran his fingers through his hair. It was fairly short and mostly gray. The tee he'd chosen sported a logo from a local restaurant and was the same color gray as his gym shorts. "That's crazy."

"When you saw them," Billie went on, "did everything appear to be okay? Nothing struck you as peculiar or out of place?"

"The man," Mr. Sowell explained, "came to the door.

He was nice. Gave me an extra good tip. That's always welcome."

"Did you see the woman, Briana?" Billie asked.

He nodded. "Yeah. She was on the sofa watching television." His face scrunched in concentration. "I think she said something about being glad I arrived so quickly because she was starved."

"Was there anyone else at the cabin or was it just the two of them?"

Mr. Sowell shook his head. "I didn't see no one else. Just those two."

Billie asked, "Did you notice what they were wearing?"

"He…" Mr. Sowell hesitated. "I think he had on jeans and a tee with some baseball team on it. I can't recall which one. She never got up but whatever she was wearing had these—" he touched his shoulder "—spaghetti-like straps. I think that's what you call them."

"Did they seem calm? Happy?" Billie prodded. "You didn't notice any tension? No black eyes or bruises?"

Mr. Sowell frowned. "No. They seemed normal." He shrugged. "You know, hungry. Happy, I guess. Relaxed for sure." His chin lifted as if he'd just remembered something else. "And she smiled at me. I remember that." His head bobbed up and down. "She had a nice smile."

When Billie didn't ask another question, Charly did. "Mr. Sowell, did you notice any other vehicles? I'm sure you've delivered to the retreat before. Generally, there's one vehicle at each parking area. Did you see anyplace as you were driving through where there was an extra vehicle? Maybe you saw someone coming in as you left or coming out as you arrived."

He appeared to think on the question for a bit. Then he met her gaze. "I didn't see any other vehicle coming or going. I noticed the parked ones but don't remember if there was more than one at each spot. Sorry."

"You've been very helpful, Mr. Sowell." Billie handed him a business card. "Please call me if you think of anything else or if you hear anything about my sister and her husband. I'm really worried, Mr. Sowell."

He studied the card a moment before meeting Billie's gaze. "I will. For sure. I'm sorry to hear of your troubles."

They were outside and back in the SUV before Charly spoke again. "What now?"

"Now we drive out to the location where the SUV was found." Once he had backed out of the Sowell driveway and was rolling forward, he asked, "Do you know the place the sheriff mentioned?"

"Sure. There's a lot of tourist traffic there. They must have pushed the SUV into the water at night. Otherwise, someone would have seen them."

"We'll have a look and then—" he glanced at her as he braked for a traffic light "—we'll check out the houses on the road where Briana's tracks ended."

"Good plan." Though Charly held out little hope about any potential video of the vehicle that drove away with the kidnap victims, she was willing to pursue the possibility.

No need to remind Billie about that. He wanted to find his sister. Charly would do whatever necessary to help.

When there seemed to be nowhere to go on a case, her father always said you just beat the bushes until something popped up.

At this point, she decided it was time to call Shelly

Phillips, her fallback plan she used from time to time to cover the office and clean the rest of the cabins. Charly was pretty sure she wasn't going to have time to do the work on her agenda and to help Billie as well. And this—finding the missing couple—was top priority.

Like he'd said, time was their enemy.

Chapter Five

Boat Ramp
Sunset Drive, 2:00 p.m.

The rental Briana and her husband had used was sent into the water at the boat launch near the corner of Henry Street and Sunset Drive. Charly watched the strand of yellow crime-scene tape flap in the scarce breeze. It dangled low across the entrance, not really blocking anything. Just an impotent warning that something untoward had happened here.

Unlike Charly, Billie didn't hesitate. He stepped over the tape and walked all the way to the water's edge. There was no litter lying about. No cigarette butts. Nothing that would provide any evidence of what had transpired here. There were no cameras nearby. A visit to the two homes that faced the area gave them nothing. No one had seen or heard anything between Saturday night after eight and Tuesday morning. No doorbell video cameras or other security-type cameras in either location.

He set his hands on his hips and turned to her. "Seems an odd place for a dump site." He gestured to the homes nearby. "Actually a risky location when you consider all the possibilities for being seen around this section of the water. I said as much to Sheriff Malone."

"They were either lazy," Charly agreed, "or in a hurry."

A smile tugged at the corners of his mouth, making her strangely happy. When was the last time a simple smile had given her such a lift?

More than three years ago.

She blinked away the thought.

"Or unafraid."

"Also a possibility," she agreed.

He took one last look around. "Unless you have another idea about this location, I'd like to get started checking in with the houses on the road that runs in front of your retreat?"

He'd said this before, maybe twice. He was really hoping to find something. She wasn't going to suggest otherwise.

"This is your investigation," she reminded him. "I'm happy to help with whatever you think we need to do but I would suggest we grab some lunch first so we don't end up running out of steam before we're finished."

"Good point." He headed for the SUV and Charly followed.

She considered the dump location of the SUV as she walked, keeping pace with this man with whom she'd formed an alliance to find the missing couple. The woman was his sister, the man his new brother-in-law; he had a serious motive for wanting to make this happen as quickly as possible. She did as well, only it wasn't anywhere near as important as his. Finding these people was first and foremost important from a purely human perspective. The fact that the disappearance happened at her retreat was a distant second for helping to solve the mystery. Of course she didn't want this to become a reason people stopped choosing her retreat. That said, she couldn't imagine how she would feel if her sister were missing.

The idea was one she never wanted to have to face.

"I'm thinking," she said as she settled into the passenger seat, "this feels too convenient to have been out-of-towners." She fastened her seat belt. "Think about it. Someone coming from some other location would scout out the best spots for doing their work. Someone local—maybe someone who knew this area well, lived around here or something—would feel more comfortable taking the risk of a plain sight dump location."

He pulled out on Sunset and headed into the turn onto Henry. "Have I mentioned that you would make a hell of a good investigator?"

She laughed. "You may have said something along those lines. I guess some of the kid comes out in me when I start trying to solve a mystery."

As much as she'd loved her mother and baking cookies with her on Sunday afternoons, she had adored spending time on a case with her father. Even now, her sister would insist that Charly had been the daddy's girl and she the mother's.

"Where would you like to get food?" He glanced at her. "Fast preferably."

"JJ's. It's a great local place. Good burgers. There's a drive-through and it's close, right on Gunter Avenue."

"Burgers work for me as long as they have good fries." He shot her a grin. "If that works for you."

She liked his smile. Liked him. He was easy to be around, even though they barely knew each other. She rarely met people she felt so comfortable with so quickly. Admittedly, she had plenty of friends, neighbors, acquaintances. But no one who made her feel young again. She rolled her eyes at herself. *Young* wasn't the right word. He made her feel...*alive.*

Moving past the foolish thought, she concurred, "Fries are a requirement." She studied him a moment. "You seem to have gotten past the fact that the sheriff left you out of the press conference."

"Nothing to be done about it now." He glanced at her. "Besides, I'm happy for him to take all the glory as long as we find my sister and her husband safe and sound."

Charly faced forward. Billie was a nice guy. She wondered how far he would have to be pushed before the nice went away.

Maybe she didn't want to know.

A QUICK DETOUR to JJ's and they were headed for Bakers Chapel Road. The road that bordered the width of Charly's retreat ran from Conners Island Parkway to Highway 431. At the spot where Bakers Chapel Lane split off was the turn, Deep Woods Trail, into Bradly Retreat. Along the southwest end of Bakers Chapel Road were a few scattered houses and a church or two. On the northeast end, just beyond the turn to her place, was an equipment rental shop. The space between the structures was thickly wooded. On her side of the road was forest all the way down to the water.

Her father had inherited the land that would eventually become incredibly valuable from his own father. She'd had offers to buy her out numerous times. But Charly wouldn't budge no matter how good the offer. This was home and she intended to stay right here until…forever. She had no desire to live anywhere else. Her sister had been happy to sell her half of their inheritance to Charly. Equally important, she had patiently waited until Charly could manage the loan—a whole five years after their parents' deaths. In truth, that feat had only been possible with Alex's help.

Since they had opted to start on the northeast end of Bakers Chapel Road, their first stop was at the equipment rental. With its high wire fences, surely there were cameras as well. Charly had been here before when she had needed a backhoe. Generally, any work that required big equipment had been Alex's domain. But Charly knew the owner. He'd grown up in Guntersville as well. Though he was closer to her sister's age than Charly's. Really, it was a small town where everyone knew everyone else. The influx of tourists and out-of-towners was more seasonal. There were plenty of rich folks who lived in nearby Madison County who built big weekend houses wherever land could be bought anywhere near the water. But few lived here full-time.

As she and Billie approached the rental shop, her hopes about cameras were confirmed. There were three on each of the two sides she could see. Most likely the other two sides would have the same. This was good. Hopefully.

There was only one person behind the counter when they entered the building. The cool air was a welcome reprieve from the July heat. Charly knew Vince Cox, the owner of the company, but the man behind the counter wasn't Vince. Since she had no influence with this guy, she stood by and let Billie make an intro.

She smiled to herself at the idea she couldn't seem to remember that he was the investigator, and she was just the person who'd rented a cabin to his sister and her husband. She kind of liked this investigator gig. Maybe she really had missed her calling. Nah. The idea of being an investigator was intriguing, but she liked her current life just fine. She wouldn't leave Bradly Retreat.

Billie flashed his credentials to the man behind the counter. "We're looking for a man and woman who were abducted from the Bradly Retreat area. We have reason to believe they were taken in a vehicle that waited on this road and may have passed right by your shop. It would be a great help if we could have a look at your video security footage."

The man, twenty-five or six, looked from Billie to Charly and back. "I'd have to ask the owner."

"Tell him," Charly spoke up, "that Charly Nix needs his help with this. It could make all the difference in whether we find this couple."

The man, Winston, according to the name tag on his shirt, nodded. "Sure thing." He walked into the office behind the counter and made the call.

While they waited Billie glanced around the showroom. There wasn't so much inside, but outside was a huge array of equipment. Just about anything you could need for digging or reaching the top of a building or tree.

"There's a church a little farther up the road then a house or two," she said, drawing his attention. "I'm thinking this is our best bet."

"If his cameras are working and assuming the video

doesn't overwrite itself every day," he pointed out as he braced his forearms on the counter.

She hadn't considered those possibilities. So much for armchair investigating.

"It would help a lot," he went on, more to himself than to her, "just to know when they were taken."

She imagined that his concern for his sister's safety had escalated significantly after the find of the vehicle. He kept his feelings close to the vest, but his eyes told the story.

"You said someone was going to let you know about when and where they used their credit cards." Maybe he would hear from that source soon. It was possible that alone would narrow down the time frame considerably. Might even help find them…maybe.

He checked his cell phone. "I should have that anytime now."

Winston exited the office and joined them at the counter. "You're in luck," he announced, then looked straight at Charly. "Vince said I should give you whatever you need." He winked. "He also said you should let him know if he can help in any way whatsoever."

Charly managed a grateful smile. "Thanks."

Winston jerked his head toward the office. "The storage room is behind the office. We have the security station set up there."

Billie and Charly followed him beyond the office and into a large storage room. An even larger area stored some of the equipment. Lots of smaller equipment pieces, like compressors and generators and all manner of tools. Behind the building was where the big earthmoving and lift equipment waited—inside yet another fence.

Winston explained the steps required to select a date to view the footage and then to move on to the next date. "You just tap this button. And the footage will move along pretty quickly until there's movement then it slows to a crawl. That way you don't have to sit through all those hours."

"Thanks." Billie waited for Charly to take a seat before taking the one directly in front of the screen. "It pays to know people," he said.

"Guess so." She didn't mention that Vince had asked her to dinner on several occasions in the past year, but she just hadn't been able to take him up on the offer. He was a very nice man. Nice-looking, too. But he had been friends with Alex and it just didn't feel right.

Rather than start with Saturday night, Billie selected Friday so he could watch Briana and Martin arrive. Winston was right. As soon as there was movement picked up in the camera's field of vision, the fast-forward-style speed slowed to almost slow motion. Their faces weren't really clear since they had come from the Huntsville direction and the angle of the camera wasn't optimal, but it was obvious they were both in the vehicle. They drove on past. The turn onto Deep Woods Trail was out of the camera's reach.

"Is there a story there?"

His voice startled her. She was so intent on the screen and thinking about the missing couple that she kind of jumped when he spoke. "I'm sorry. What?"

"With you and the guy who owns the place—Vince? Is there a story there?"

Charly sighed. "He and my husband were very good friends. Whenever Alex needed something bigger than a shovel or an extension ladder, Vince was always helping out. When Vince needed an electrician or plumber, Alex was always available. They were good friends." She hesitated. "We all were."

"That makes any other kind of relationship awkward," he suggested.

"Yeah. I mean Vince's a really nice guy." She shrugged. "Still offers to help with anything I need. I guess I just can't go there."

"I get it." Billie nodded, his attention on the screen. "I read up on you," he admitted, "on the way here."

"Really?" She should have known this. He was a PI. Finding information on people was his business.

"You built the retreat right out of high school—after your parents' deaths. Not long after that you married a local guy who helped you pursue your dream."

"My parents' dream," she countered. "They had dreamed of building the retreat for as long as I can remember."

"And you—" he glanced at her "—made sure it happened." He watched the footage going by on the screen. "Your husband died three years ago and even then you kept the dream going."

Wow. He'd gotten all that during a single flight.

"Since I know basically nothing about you, how about you tell me some things. Like, are you married?" She hadn't even considered whether he was or not until now. A discreet glance at his left hand showed no ring but that wasn't always an indicator.

Something about the way he'd dropped everything and rushed here made her assume he was single. Life was more complicated when you were married, particularly if you had kids. You couldn't just rush off without making arrangements. But this was his sister. Any significant other would surely understand the need and take care of things back home.

"I am not." He sent her a look that said he was perfectly satisfied with that answer and intended to offer no other details.

She bit her tongue to prevent asking why. He seemed to be around her age. Surely, there was a particular someone. She wasn't asking that, either, given he seemed not to want to indulge more.

"I had a serious relationship about seven years ago," he said to her surprise and as if her other question had reached him by osmosis. "But it didn't work out and there's been no one serious since."

"No reason to rush." It was the only response she could think to give. Not exactly original but it was better than saying nothing.

"You haven't dated anyone since your husband died?"

He looked at her…his very blue eyes quite serious. Nice eyes to go with that nice smile. "I have not. I've been super-busy and I guess I just haven't met anyone."

This was true. She never went anywhere to meet anyone. She only went to places like the market or the hardware store. The people she encountered were all friends she and Alex shared during their twelve-year marriage. Somehow, she just couldn't see a relationship with anyone like that. Or maybe she just hadn't been ready. She probably still wasn't.

"No one who grabbed your attention, huh?" he said without looking at her this time.

"Nope," she insisted in her firmest voice.

The tingle started deep in her belly and belied the single word. Okay, so she was sort of attracted to this guy but he had used past tense when he asked the question so that meant he didn't count since he was present, right? She focused on the monitor with that footage of Bakers Chapel Road clicking by. The mere idea was foolish really. And maybe that was why she was attracted to this stranger who had suddenly invaded her life. He wouldn't be here long. The situation surrounding his arrival was troubling and extremely stressful.

It made perfect sense.

He would be leaving and she wouldn't have to figure out how to end *it*. Not that there was an *it* right now. On top of that, the intensity of the situation had emotions on overload.

"You will when you're ready." He said this with absolutely no doubt in his tone.

She was glad one of them was so sure. But she was more glad to be moving on from the subject.

Her attention fully fixed on the reason they were here, she noted that the footage showed Friday was nothing but the arrival of the newlyweds. Saturday was a big nothing reel. But then Sunday revealed the two of them leaving in the white SUV around ten that morning. Coming from the opposite direction gave a better look at their faces. Both were smiling. A few hours later they returned. Then the evening and overnight hours of nothing relevant. He switched to Monday.

"If they used their credit cards—" he glanced at her "—then we should be able to determine where they went on Sunday."

"Most of the shops are closed on Sunday mornings,"

she pointed out. "Considering how long they were gone they may have driven to Scottsboro or just to a local restaurant to have lunch. Maybe they lingered over dessert." Charly considered the many activities available in the area. "They may have taken a boat ride or gone fishing. Skiing. Parasailing."

"Any of that," Billie pointed out, "would make my sister very happy."

Briana sounded like a fun girl. Charly considered that she had stopped bothering with any sort of fun activity nearly four years ago—after Alex was diagnosed. Cancer sucked. Especially when you were so young. She refused extra help until near the end when specialized care was essential. She had wanted to take care of him. He'd begged her to not spend all her time with him but there had been no changing her mind. Shelly Phillips was happy to pick up the slack taking care of the retreat so Charly could focus on Alex.

The footage slowed again. Charly snapped back to the here and now. This time it was Monday night. Nine o'clock. Tension rippled through her. She leaned closer to the screen. Billie did the same.

The white SUV that Briana and Martin had rented departed the retreat going in that northwesterly direction that took them right past this location and the cameras. Charly's heart stumbled when she saw a man—not Martin—behind the wheel. There was no one in the passenger seat. Seeing the man's face was impossible with the bill of that baseball cap he wore pulled so low.

She and Billie sat silently staring at the screen, as if waiting for the other shoe to drop.

The footage sped up again. Charly had just managed

a breath when that shoe dropped. The footage slowed once more. At nine-fifty a black SUV, not as fancy as the one Billie drove, more generic, drove through the field of view of the cameras. Again, there appeared to be only the one person in the vehicle. Male, the driver. He, too, wore a baseball cap pulled low so his facial features weren't visible. If there was anyone else in the SUV, they couldn't be seen.

Billie made note of the time when the two SUVs appeared on the footage and then he ran through the rest of the footage all the way until Tuesday afternoon when he arrived.

"They had to be in that black SUV," Charly said, her throat dry, her body tense with equal measures frustration and fear.

"They came from the direction where her heel impressions ended," he said, his voice quiet, calm…too calm.

"Right."

"If we can find a camera on that end of Bakers Chapel," he continued, "maybe we can get a license plate."

Anticipation had her heart kicking harder into gear. "Maybe. Of course there are all the usual reasons we might not be able to see it on a quick pass-by on a home camera. Like mud or something blocking it. But we can hope."

He breathed a laugh. "We can." He turned his attention back to the computer monitor. "Let me download a copy of Monday's footage and email it to myself and we'll see what we can find down the road."

While his fingers flew across the keys, Charly thought of the newly married couple. What had happened to them? Had they been bound and gagged in the back of that SUV? Her heart thumped harder and harder until she wanted to scream. Nearly forty-eight hours. Briana and Martin had been taken approximately forty-three hours ago.

What was it her father always used to say? *The first forty-eight were critical.* Those fleeting hours could make all the difference. The chances of being found alive reduced dramatically after that.

There were only five hours left in that critical time frame.

Chapter Six

Bradly Retreat
Deep Woods Trail, 7:00 p.m.

The two houses and the church were a no-go for security cameras of any sort. Charly hadn't pinned much hope on the possibility, but it had been worth a check. From there they had gone to the sheriff's office and told him what they'd found on the security footage at Vince's Equipment Rental.

Sheriff Malone had called Vince personally and ordered a copy of the footage from Friday until now delivered to his email so that he could have a look for himself. Seemed a waste of time to Charly but then maybe another pair of eyes was a good thing. He might recognize the black SUV or the driver, though the possibility was highly unlikely. The details were far too vague.

Charly pulled the baking sheet from the oven and checked the status of the bacon. She wasn't much of a cook. She'd gotten used to Alex reigning over the kitchen. He had loved to cook so she never bothered. She could bake a mean chocolate chip cookie thanks to her mother. The making of good coffee she had mastered, as well as BLT sandwiches. But that was about the extent of her culinary repertoire.

Kind of sad but she didn't generally let it bother her because she didn't usually have company who hung around for a meal with her. She was far more experienced in selecting ready-to-eat products for her guests and herself. Life was less complicated that way. And cleanup was a breeze.

Billie appeared at the sink with a large tomato. He rinsed it and grabbed a knife from the block to slice it. Okay, so there was one other thing she was pretty good at. Growing stuff—the easy stuff. Her father had planted an orchard when she was a little girl. It was closer to the entrance since the natural woods were thinner there. Apples, pears, peaches, cherries—all the trees produced an abundance of fruit. Thankfully, in all the years she had been running the place, she had not lost a single tree. On the sunny side of her back deck she planted a few items in pots. Tomatoes, lettuce, cucumbers and a couple of varieties of peppers as well as her favorite herbs. She kept that going until frost. It made her feel better about her lack of culinary skills. For years now, she had planted lavender wherever it would grow. She loved adding fresh lavender to the cabins between guests. The guests appeared to love it as well.

"You're doing a great job on that tomato," she commented just to break the silence.

He glanced up as he finished slicing. "I do have my kitchen talents." With that, he opened the fridge and grabbed a handful of lettuce from the cloth bag and placed it on the plate next to the tomatoes.

"Like I told you, I'm afraid my talents in the kitchen

are quite limited." He might as well know this up front in case he planned on eating with her during his stay.

The question of how long it would take to find his sister and her husband expanded in her brain. The couple might never be found. She swallowed hard. Not that she minded having him here—not at all, in fact—but that would mean she would have to watch him go through that nightmare. The uncertainty. The defeat. The painful final reality.

"But," he said with one of those smiles that seemed so easy and…very nice to look at, "you obviously have other related skills. I scoped out your little garden." He leaned against the sink now, arms folded over his chest. "Not bad for someone who doesn't like to cook."

"Thanks." She frowned. "I think."

"Your friend, Shelly, finished the cleanup of the cabins."

"And the restocking and the laundry." Thank God for Shelly. "If I can't be here she'll check in the new guests on Friday." Maybe she should have asked her to do a supply run as well. Restocks always depleted most of her inventory. She didn't like waiting to replenish those shelves.

He stared at the floor. Didn't take a mind reader to recognize he likely hoped his sister would be found before then. At this point, Charly had her doubts. This was looking far more sinister than before. There was no mistake about dates. No decision by the couple to take a little side trip. This was an abduction. No question.

"Sheriff Malone didn't mention any ideas on the investigation?" She shrugged. "He hasn't found anything on his end?"

In the middle of their meeting she'd had to take a call from her sister, which was a good thing—she loved hearing from Jen but she'd missed the rest of whatever the sheriff had to say. Since Billie hadn't said anything on the drive back here, she hadn't wanted to ask. If new evidence had been found to suggest the worst, she figured he would tell her when he was ready.

Billie shook his head, his lips tight with frustration. "But I did some deeper digging in the wee hours of the morning, which is partly why I didn't really sleep, and I spotted a pattern." He exhaled a big breath. "Well, calling it a pattern might be a stretch. The instances were few and far between, but I found about seven similar incidents over the past sixteen years. I tried to look back further but I didn't find anything that met the same criteria beyond that point."

"What exactly did you find?" She reached into the oven and removed the pan. Folding back the foil, she was pleased to see the bacon was nicely browned but not burned. Moving it from the foil to a plate where a paper towel would allow it to drain, she resisted the urge to ask why he hadn't mentioned his search earlier today. Whatever his reason, he appeared ready to talk now.

He turned around to face the counter as if he intended to help. She held up a hand. "You talk, I'll make the sandwiches."

"Is that code for get out of my way?" he asked with his hands up.

"It is." She laughed and shooed him away with a hand. "The BLT is my specialty."

A deep chuckle as he moved to the far end of the

counter had her grinning at him. After bracing a hip there, he said, "Like I said, I couldn't sleep so I was looking for missing persons reports from the area," he explained. "There's quite a few every year in the tri-county area of Marshall, Madison and Jackson. Sadly, that's not unusual. It's the same in most places. Someone disappears because they want to or are forced to. Reports are filed. In the end, the results are mixed."

"Some are never found," she offered as she placed the bread on the plates. "Others show up in another town leading their lives as if nothing happened."

"Some are dead." He said the part no one wanted to hear.

No one wanted that end, either. She placed the bacon on one side of the bread, then added mustard. "Oh shoot!" She looked to her guest, who appeared deep in thought. "I forgot to ask if you liked mayo or mustard."

He flashed a smile that didn't reach his eyes. "Either one works for me."

She returned the smile, hers likely as feeble as his. "You were saying."

"I narrowed the results down to this specific area and I found seven over a sixteen-year period."

"So our fair city has had seven disappearances over the past sixteen years?" Frankly, she had expected the number to be higher. She added the tomatoes and lettuce and the other slices of bread.

"Seven unresolved disappearances of victims who meet certain criteria."

Okay, so obviously, more disappearances but some were solved. Or were different, depending on what he meant by criteria. Not that Guntersville was a bad place to live. It was great. But the world wasn't such a safe place as when she'd been a kid. People went missing all the time. Sometimes even in the best places. It was really important to always be vigilant even in your hometown.

"What are the criteria you mentioned?" She passed a plate to him. "Beer? Cola? Water?"

He took the plate. Studied the sandwich placed in the middle. "A beer would be nice."

Her pulse jumped at the realization that she might not even have any beer. Alex had liked beer. The offer was automatic. She prowled through the fridge, certain she was going to have to retract the offer, then found a single bottle of Alex's favorite. Whew.

"Here you go." She passed it to him. Hoped it wouldn't be bad. It had likely been in there for three years. Maybe four.

Why in the world had she offered him a beer? It wasn't like he was the first person she'd shared a meal with in her own kitchen.

No...he was just the first *man* she had shared a meal with in her own kitchen.

And Alex had loved the occasional beer.

This man was not Alex, she reminded herself. He was not a potential boyfriend. He was a man desperate to find his sister, who needed company in this unfamiliar place.

Charly shook off the annoying thoughts, grabbed a cola and sat down at the table. She didn't wait for him to answer the question she'd tossed out about his middle-of-the-night research. She ate. Mostly because the scent of the bacon cooking had reminded her that she was starving.

"In all seven cases," he said after indulging in a bite himself, "the victim was female. In two of the cases, a male partner—either boyfriend or husband—went missing as well."

Wow. Talk about similarities. "Ages? Any other statistics on the victims?"

"All seven were Caucasian. All of the seven females had blond hair like Briana. One male had dark hair, the other blond. The males were also Caucasian. All in their mid-to-late twenties. Those seven cases are the only ones from the Guntersville area that remain unsolved."

She chewed slowly as she considered all that he'd said. "Were any of the seven cases people from the area?" She figured the answer was no since she would certainly recall someone local disappearing and never being found. Well, except maybe for during the time Alex was sick. She had been a wreck and totally off the grid as far as news went.

"None. All were folks who had come to the area for a vacation."

Like his sister and her husband. Her heart reacted to the reality of what he was saying.

"Sixteen years, seven cases with nine victims," she said aloud, mostly to herself. "Is that a lot for an area this size?"

He took a swallow of his beer. Since he didn't make a face she assumed the drink was still good. "The number isn't a lot, but the specificity is significant. Seven blonde white women, two with partners. Now there's Briana, a blonde white woman, with her husband. I call that a pattern."

"Wow." Charly was taken aback by the statistics as well when he laid them out that way. "Should we ask Sheriff Malone about this?"

Not something she looked forward to. Other than being a decent sheriff, one thing she knew about the man: He did not like to be called out on his work record. He preferred the praise for a job well done. She remembered her father saying that about him when he was sheriff and Tully Malone was the chief deputy.

"Let's talk about Sheriff Malone," Billie suggested. He'd finished off his sandwich and was concentrating on his beer but taking his time.

Alex had done that. As much as he loved beer—and he did—he said showing his ass once in college was enough to set him right about how to handle alcohol. He had taken his time with any alcoholic beverage and never overindulged.

"What would you like to know?" She popped the last bite of BLT into her mouth. So good, even if she did say so herself.

"The usual stats were easy to find." He braced his forearms on the table. "Fifty years old. Married three times, two kids—one each with the first two wives. Fairly good record on the job, which he has held for sixteen years. There have been some complaints but not so many. The usual stuff. Unfair with certain cases. A couple of accusations about brutality on the part of some of his deputies. Not so much in light of the length of his career and how touristy the area is."

There was plenty Charly could say but she weighed her words. What Billie was asking for were facts, not personal opinions. At least that was what she thought he wanted to hear.

"He was about the age I am now when my father died," Charly said first. "He was arrogant, cocky, hardheaded and bucking for a promotion. Those are things my father said to my mother on more than one occasion. I was too young to notice or to care. I had just turned eighteen. It was the final weeks of my senior year of high school, and I was focused on going away to college in the fall."

He watched her as she spoke. Analyzing her, she decided. She couldn't help wondering what he thought. She leaned back in her chair and let her hands rest in her lap. Oddly enough, she wasn't nervous. But she did wonder what he would ask next as if their conversation was some sort of foreplay.

Foolish, Charly. No. Desperate *was the word.*

"You don't recall anyone disappearing while you were growing up?"

Easy question. "I do. I distinctly remember four cases. My father found them each time." She hesitated. A frown furrowed its way across her brow. "There was a case that happened not long before he…died. I don't think that one was ever solved." A memory pinged her, and her mouth opened in surprise. "It was a blonde woman. White. Youngish. Everyone over twenty seemed old to me in those days. But then my parents…died and I don't know what happened with that case."

His gaze seemed somehow more intent now. Bored into her as if he might see what was in her memory for himself. "Do you remember a name?"

"Fran…something. Frances." She scrubbed at her forehead, then she recalled. "Francesca. Francesca Andrews."

The frown was back, tugging at her brow. "I don't think she was ever found. Does that make eight?"

He nodded. "It does if she wasn't found. I didn't find her in my search. Let's check her age and see if she was found." He used his cell to google any available information on the woman.

Blond hair and blue eyes flashed in Charly's mind. The image of the woman's photo in the paper followed.

"Francesca Andrews," Billie said. "She went missing just as you said." His gaze met hers. "Like the other blonde women, she was a visitor to the area. But she didn't show up in my search because she was found." His focus returned to his phone. He frowned. "Now this is a bizarre twist." His gaze met Charly's once more. "She went missing again two months later—from her hometown of Nashville, Tennessee."

Her anxiety level soared. After her father died. "That is bizarre. What are you thinking?"

"Has there ever been talk of human trafficking issues in the area?" He set his phone aside. "In my research on the flight here, I found the topic discussed occasionally on one website or the other. But nothing that gave me pause. Now that I'm here I can see how this would be the perfect location for that sort of thing. Drug smuggling and the like. Guntersville is easy access to the Tennessee River. Getting someone or thing out of the city on a boat in the middle of the night would be relatively easy."

"We had plenty of that," she agreed. "The drug smuggling. My father set up a task force when I was in eighth grade and stamped out a lot of the drugs coming in. It hasn't been big in the news around here since that time. Like most places, I hear the talk of human trafficking."

She'd heard all the issues that appeared to be affecting the country as a whole, but nothing as far as a hot spot in Guntersville or anything like that. Not since she was in junior high school anyway. Then again, maybe the bad guys had just gotten better at evading the law and hiding their work.

"The subject of human trafficking has come up," she agreed, "but no specific or big problems here to my knowledge." She planted her elbows on the table and set her chin in her hands. "I might not be the best person to ask. Mostly when I'm watching news it's about the weather."

"A lot of people don't like to watch the news," he said, letting her off the hook. "But I think it's worth a close look because Briana and Martin's disappearance would make number eight in sixteen years—nine if you count Francesca—that fit a specific criteria. Nashville isn't that far from here and she fits the profile. The fact that all the cases fall into the same MO is relevant to me. In a big way. The trouble is that the feedback from my agency's contact in the Bureau is that local law enforcement doesn't treat it like a big deal. In two instances it wasn't even reported to them."

Charly's heart started to beat a little faster. "By Bureau I assume you mean the FBI."

"I do. Apparently, Sheriff Malone isn't always a team player when it comes to what he refers to as outside interference."

Not surprised, Charly shook her head. "I can see that. My father had trouble with him when he was sheriff and Tully was a deputy."

"Malone took over after your father's death."

Charly nodded. "He was interim sheriff until an election, and he's held the position since."

"He must be popular with the voters," Billie suggested.

"To some degree, yes. But honestly, no one capable of beating him ever runs." Charly wasn't sure why that was the case so she opted not to give her opinion.

"He and your father didn't get along?"

She gave a dry half laugh. "My father said he was a hothead who wasn't as thorough as he should be. But then my father was persnickety."

"Your parents' murders were never solved."

"They were not." A knot formed instantly in her gut at the subject. Talking about her parents' deaths always did that. "When the insurance money came, Jen and I hired a private investigator, but he had no better luck than the sheriff's department or the Alabama Bureau of Investigations. They were driving home and for whatever reason stopped on the road and were shot where they sat in the family car."

Dread settled heavily on her chest. It was the same every time she allowed those memories to slip in. She had been visiting Jen but could imagine the details as vividly as if she had been in the car with them. Had she not been away, she probably would have been.

"No one your father had put away had sufficient motive to go to such an extreme for revenge?"

His gaze was doing that probing thing again as if he were trying to see right through her. To analyze what she was thinking.

"There were plenty who had motive but they were all either in jail or had moved away or I guess had an alibi."

Really, those days were a bit of a blur. To lose both parents in one fell swoop was hard to muddle through at such a young age.

"You were visiting your sister," he said. "I think I read something about that in one of the articles I found."

"Yes. At Sanford in Birmingham. I was supposed to go there in the fall that year but…after what happened, someone had to stay here and take care of things."

She remembered the argument with her sister. She hadn't wanted Charly to stay. It certainly hadn't been about the money that the sale of this place would have brought at the time. It was about fear that something would happen to her, too. But Charly had been determined to see her parents' dream through to fruition.

"Have you hired anyone else to look into the case?" he asked. "Over the years, I mean."

"I did once about seven years ago." She shook her head. "But he hit a wall, too. Alex helped me decide to let it go after that. It drove me crazy for a long time that their killer is still out there—if he's not dead by now or in prison for some other crime. But I learned to live with it."

"If you wouldn't mind," he said, his voice gentle, his gaze comforting, "I can look into the case. See if we can find something the others missed."

A long-dead hope stirred. "That would be great." Wow. The idea that the Colby Agency would look into the case startled her. They might actually find the truth. Except…it had been a really long time. Sixteen years. "Do you think it's possible to find the truth after so long?"

A smile slid across his lips. "The truth has always been there and always will be. It's just a matter of turning over the right rock to find where it has been hiding."

Anticipation seared through her. She tamped it back. “But first,” she said, to steady her runaway hopes, “you have to find your sister and her husband.”

His smile faded. “I will find them. I won’t stop until I do.”

Chapter Seven

Thursday, July 9

Piggly Wiggly
Sunset Drive, 9:15 a.m.

Charly wasn't a big fan of shopping. She would much rather be back home working at the retreat, weeding the flowerbeds her mother had put in decades ago or some other hands-on maintenance. Thank God the plants were the sort that came back every year. Peonies and what her mother had called cone flowers. The other varieties Charly wasn't sure about, but those two had been her mother's favorites. She remembered those well.

She didn't even mind the cleaning of the cabins. It made her happy. Probably best not to tell anyone else about her love of cleaning. The task wasn't usually something folks liked to do. Laundry was another mundane activity that made her happy. Relaxed her. Maybe it was because she was in control of the results and the results rarely let her down.

More of the snack bars that seemed to go over so well with her guests went into her cart. The paper goods aisle was next. Paper towels and toilet paper. She was low on both. She used cloth napkins because she hated using so much paper. One of these days she intended to attempt moving to reusable paper towels as well. Just not today.

Lastly, she needed to make her way to the produce department. First, she took her full cart up front and left it next to the line of cash registers. She waved to Wanda Briggs, a longtime head cashier at the Pig, as everyone called it. Wanda gave Charly a nod, letting her know it was okay to leave the cart until she was finished.

"How many cases of water you need?" Wanda asked. "I'll have someone ready to load it for you."

"Four, please. Thanks." Charly gave her a thumbs-up.

Once she had snagged another cart, Charly headed to produce. Another favorite of her guests was the fruit baskets she prepared. So far, she hadn't heard the first complaint and she'd been doing it for years. Maybe the secret was the small box of chocolates she tucked in every basket.

As for the fruit, the bananas were the trickiest. But over the years she had refined her ability to select the best level of ripeness to ensure they lasted through the weekend.

"Charly, how are you doing?"

Charly looked up to find Laney Rogers and her cart nose to nose with her own. The tilt of her lips upward was automatic, no matter that she could have gone the rest of her life without bumping into the other woman. Laney was thirty or so years older than Charly and operated the Lost in the Woods Getaway. She claimed to have come up with the idea of cabins combined with a salon that offered a host of spa services. She was probably right about that. Most folks who came for fishing and hiking in the woods weren't exactly the right customer base for spas in Charly's opinion. Then again, what did she know? Laney had been in business for thirty-odd years. Had won business of the year two or three times. She had to be doing something right.

"I'm good. And you?" Keeping the smile in place was particularly hard this morning.

"Lord," she said, putting a hand to her chest, "if we get any busier I don't know what we'll do." Her expression shifted to a pout. "I was so sorry to hear about what happened to that couple staying at your place. I hope it doesn't hurt business for the rest of the summer. You know we had that young woman, Francesca Andrews, who went missing all those years ago. It was a mess until they found her."

For whatever reason, Charly hadn't realized the woman who'd gone missing had been staying at the Lost in the Woods Getaway. She'd likely known it at the time, but sixteen years was a long time and she had been found—at least the first time.

"We're hoping for the best," Charly replied.

Laney looked confused and Charly realized her mistake. There was only *her*, no we. She was alone. Lived alone. Ran the retreat alone for the most part. She glanced at her cart. Shopped for her guests alone.

"I mean—" she shifted her attention back to Laney "—me and the…the family of the missing couple, of course."

Laney adopted a knowing look. "I hear the missing bride's brother is some big-time private investigator. Has he given you any trouble? I imagine he's pushing you and the sheriff to find his sister. Is it true there are still no leads?"

Some folks loved gossip. Thrived on it. Laney was one of them. She didn't mean any harm really, Charly's mother had always said. But Charly wasn't so sure. In recent years, Charly had noticed an uptick of gossip about all the other lodging operations around town. Shelly insisted it was coming from Laney since her bookings were down. Whatever the case, Charly didn't want to give the woman any additional fodder about her troubles.

"He's concerned and asking lots of questions," Charly said. "That's to be expected. He's a very nice man. As for leads, you would have to ask the sheriff about that."

Laney's expression remained doubtful, but she nodded. "Good to know about the brother. As for talking to the sheriff, you know Tully. He's always too busy to talk to anyone not on his radar at any given moment."

"Well..." Charly smiled as brightly as possible. "I should get this shopping finished. I have to prepare for the next group of guests. Good to see you, Laney."

Not.

Charly finished selecting the fruits she needed and hurried to the front of the store. By the time she had paid the total, a young man appeared to help her get the purchases to her vehicle. Thankfully, he took care of the cases of bottled water.

Outside, the sun felt scorching already and it was barely ten o'clock. This was going to be a hot one. If she didn't have a million things to do she would take a dip in the lake. Maybe later tonight, if there was time.

Once she had put away her load and prepared all the fruit baskets, she would help Billie with whatever steps he wanted to take next. Or he might require her help before she did the fruit baskets. Whatever he needed. Helping to find Briana and Martin was priority one.

He hadn't called her this morning. He'd mentioned a conference call with his agency and then a trip to see the sheriff again. He hadn't invited her to join so she hadn't asked if he needed her. There were aspects of this situation in which she could be no assistance to him, but she still wanted to help. She really, really did. If for nothing other than to serve as a buffer when he spoke to any of the locals or the sheriff. She had known Tully Malone most of her life. She pretty much had him figured out. The possibility that maybe Billie didn't exactly like the way she took over the conversation when she felt compelled wasn't lost on her. It was a bad habit, she supposed. He likely wasn't accustomed to having someone else intrude into whatever he was doing on a case.

Particularly one as personal as this.

She thanked the man who had helped her load up with a nice tip and then climbed behind the steering wheel. If Billie received the list of places where the couple's credit cards had been used, they could check the businesses for cameras. Maybe determine if someone had been following them if there was video footage. Wasn't that what kidnappers did? They watched and followed their prey until they found the right opportunity to pounce?

Then again, she may have watched far too many true-crime shows.

And there she went, acting like she knew what their next step should be.

Charly had just started to back out of her slot when banging on her vehicle had her slamming on the brakes. She stared at the rearview mirror, hoping she hadn't nearly run over someone. Clear. Then another knock on the glass right next to her face made her jump.

Deputy Cohen Lathan stood outside her door, grinning like a jackass. Slumping with a combination of relief and frustration, she shoved the gearshift into Park and then powered the window down. She might have ignored him and continued backing up if not for the possibility that he might have an update on the case.

"Hey, Cohen." She tried her best to prevent the anger that tinged her voice, but it just wasn't possible.

Hands on hips, head cocked with sunglasses shielding his eyes, he studied her a moment. She barely resisted rolling her eyes.

"What have you been telling that guy from Chicago?" he demanded.

Charly drew back at the accusatory tone. "What are you talking about?"

"He showed up in the sheriff's office this morning making all kinds of accusations about missing women and unsolved cases from the past." He tore his sunglasses off. "So, I ask again, what have you been telling him? Obviously, you've got him all fired up about old cases that aren't even relevant anymore much less related to his missing sister. Geez Louise, where's your sense of community? Your loyalty?"

As much as Charly wanted to tell him exactly what she thought about his accusations and him, she recognized that it was better to go at this from a different angle. "I didn't tell him anything about any cases," she said firmly. "Everything he learned was from the internet and..." She shouldn't do this; she really shouldn't. "From the FBI.

He has major connections, and he intends to do whatever necessary to find his sister."

The fact that every ounce of blood seemed to drain out of the cocky deputy's face was almost enough to make her smile.

But Charly wasn't finished yet. Too late to turn back now. "You know he works for the Colby Agency. I looked up that agency and it's a really big deal." She widened her eyes as large as possible. "Seriously, I'm talking huge. They're looking into the case as well. Two more investigators may be showing up."

The last was total fiction but she couldn't resist.

Red replaced the pallor that had claimed his face. "Well, let them," he sneered. "We're doing everything we can with the resources we have. This ain't Chicago and we can't just pull stuff out of our—"

"I know." Charly nodded vigorously, almost feeling guilty. "I'm sure you're doing all you can." Despite the guilt, she decided to dig. "I'm sure that video footage we got from Vince Cox will be very useful."

He harrumphed. "Worthless. You can't ID a vehicle without seeing the license plate or the driver or something. That damned SUV could be from anywhere. The footage is worthless."

Exactly what she'd expected. "Well, we tried."

"More likely," Cohen argued, "the two had a big argument and she took off with someone else and then her new husband dumped their rental in the water just to spook her. Newlyweds do stupid stuff. They'll probably show up any day now and make up like nothing ever happened."

Was he serious? "May…be," she offered.

He leaned his head closer to her open window. "For all we know the two were drugged out of their minds. They could be anywhere."

Charly held her mouth shut for five seconds until she could speak without telling him what a stupid idea that was. "You never know."

He eyed her suspiciously then. "Has he—this Jagger guy—told you anything else? Or said anything about our department?"

Charly's head was moving side to side before he finished speaking. Time to smooth the feathers she'd ruffled. "I've told you everything. He's beginning to realize, I think, that ours is not your usual small-town department."

"Good. Because we're not. We're the best." He shoved his sunglasses back into place. "Now, you let me know if he tells you anything else you feel we need to know. We locals have to stick together and don't you forget it."

As if the situation couldn't get worse, Laney Rogers drove past on her way out of the parking lot. She stared a hole through Charly and the scene playing out at her front driver's-side window.

"Well, I should get the groceries home," she announced as she reached for the gearshift once more.

"Good talking to you, Charly."

She grunted something she hoped he considered to be an agreement. What was one more fib even if unspoken?

Charly watched in her rearview mirror as he sauntered away. When the coast was clear, she shifted into Reverse and exited the slot. The whole conversation had been utterly ridiculous. She hadn't exactly helped.

By the time she merged into traffic headed home, she

was outright indignant and more than a little ticked off. Had the sheriff asked him to bug Charly or had Cohen taken that duty upon himself? If she thought it would do one bit of good she would call and report him, but the sheriff would only be pleased by his deputy's loyalty.

"Jerks." Both of them.

For the next few miles, Charly focused on breathing deeply, holding and then releasing. She refused to let that bully get to her. And that was what the man was. A bully. Thankfully, most of the deputies were really nice, competent people. But there were always a few who weren't in every walk of life.

By the time she turned onto Bakers Chapel Road she had calmed down. She wrestled with the idea of whether she should tell Billie what the jerk had said. Nothing he uttered was relevant to anything or news of any sort. Not really. His words only added to the idea that Southerners could be… Well, no need to go there. She would tell Billie if the need arose.

As she approached the next curve, a vehicle roared up close behind her. She hadn't even noticed anyone in the distance of her rearview mirror. Where the heck had they come from? Suddenly, the larger vehicle was right on her bumper. SUV…black.

The driver wore a baseball cap, the bill pulled low.

The image of the driver in that video footage suddenly zoomed into vivid focus.

Fear rushed through Charly's veins and her foot pressed harder on the accelerator. She rounded the curve way too fast. The other vehicle still right on her tail. Close enough to nudge her.

She hit a pothole and the steering wheel seesawed in

her hands. She slammed on the brakes, tires squealing, and tried to straighten the front end but she was spinning.

Another glimpse of the black SUV…trees swirling around her and then she was looking into the ditch… deep ditch. Oh, God!

Her heart rocketed into her throat. She gripped the steering wheel tighter as she bounced over the terrain. Tried to slow down…tried to navigate. Not working. All sound and thought vanished…there was only the up and down motion of the vehicle and the blur of landscape.

A tree popped up in front of her. She wrestled again with the steering wheel in an attempt to swerve away from it but couldn't.

The rupture of metal interrupted the silence.

Her seat belt snapped tight.

The airbag deployed.

Her side of the SUV—right behind her—curved around the tree. Wood splintered.

She bumped against her door.

Then everything stopped and there was silence again.

Chapter Eight

Bradly Retreat
Deep Woods Trail, 10:30 a.m.

Billie knocked on the door of Charly's cabin. Her SUV wasn't parked in its usual spot, which likely meant she wasn't back from shopping, but he still knocked. When she didn't appear at the door, he dropped into one of the wooden rocking chairs on her front porch.

The conference call with Victoria and the team back at the office in Chicago had proven troubling. He was grateful for what they had been able to find, but the facts recounted to him were even more disturbing than what he'd found on his own the past couple of days. There was definitely something going on in the area. The consensus was that his sister's and her husband's abductions were related to an ongoing trafficking ring.

An ache pierced his chest. He'd had his suspicions regarding the possibility right from the beginning. But there had been no concrete proof. But now he couldn't deny the mounting evidence. He had to hand it to whoever was behind this nasty business; they were smart. There were seven counties fanned around Marshall: Madison, Jackson, Dekalb, Etowah, Blount, Cullman and Morgan. Madison and Marshall had the highest tourist activity. Marshall because of Guntersville and Madison because of Huntsville.

Like most in the country, the other seven counties had an average number of disappearances annually. Many were found; others were not. Those counties with large metropolitan areas had considerably more, of course. Marshall County's annual unfound missing stats were somewhat lower than average. The part that bothered Billie was the fact that most of those not found fit into a certain profile. White, female, light hair and eyes… like Briana.

Granted, it was the perfect location for having a wide range to choose from considering the number of tourists from all over the world who flocked here. Madison County was a close second except the bigger portion of those not found were victims of color with dark hair and eyes.

It was a sickening scenario, but Billie couldn't ignore it. Even the Bureau was watching the growing evidence that something was off with these statistics. That was the trouble with bureaucratic red tape. It always took far too long to reach a conclusion and then to decide to do something about it.

Billie wasn't waiting. He intended to act now.

Whoever was behind this operation was cherry picking victims, which could only mean one thing: He had scouts previewing those coming and going. The scout would snap photos and send them to whoever was in charge, who would in turn select the targets.

Anger burned in his gut. Someone in this town—someone people knew and possibly trusted—was the worst kind of monster. The kind who did bad things without ever getting his or her hands dirty.

Victoria had warned Billie to proceed with caution. He was in a jurisdiction where the agency had no influence, no contacts. He was on his own. They would do all possible to help get things moving at the Bureau and certainly if he needed backup, the agency would have someone en route ASAP.

At this time, that wasn't necessary. Billie had the only backup he needed. He smiled in spite of the worry twisting inside him. Charly was a pretty damned good partner.

His cell vibrated and he pulled it from his pocket. She must have known he was thinking of her. Her name appeared on the screen. He accepted the call.

"Hey, I'm back and—"

"Billie, I… I'm…" She exhaled a big breath.

The fear in her voice had him pushing to his feet. Tension rushed through him. "What's wrong, Charly? Where are you?"

"I'm on the…ah end of Bakers Chapel not far from Vince's place. I need help."

"Don't hang up," he said as he sprinted toward his SUV. "I'm on my way. Just stay on the line with me."

When he'd turned the vehicle around and headed out of the retreat, he asked, "What happened?"

"I… I was driving home from the market and a black SUV came up behind me, almost hit me so I sped up to get away. I guess I went into the curve too fast, and I hit a pothole. The next thing I knew I was crashed in the ditch."

A dozen knots had twisted in his gut. "Are you okay? Do we need to call EMS?"

"No, no… I'm okay. I think. Shaken. Just shaken."

"Are you still in the vehicle?" He pressed harder on the accelerator. Needed to get there faster.

"No. I got out. Luckily, my door wasn't damaged. I made my way up to the road."

He spotted her in the distance. "I see you," he said, the urgency nearly choking him now. "I'm almost to you."

"'Kay."

The call dropped off. He pulled to the side of the road and shoved into Park. He was out of the vehicle and rushing toward her without closing the door or shutting off the engine.

"Are you sure you're okay?" He held her by the shoulders and looked her up and down. No blood. No obvious sign of injury. He looked closely into her eyes. No dilated pupils.

"Yeah, yeah. The airbag deployed so I'm kind of…" She shrugged. "I don't know. Shaken, I guess. But I'm okay." She gestured to the ditch. "I have to get my supplies home."

Then he looked down at her vehicle in the deep ditch. She'd slammed into a tree on the driver's side. She could have injuries she didn't know about just yet.

"We're going to the ER just to be sure."

She tried to argue but he ushered her to his SUV. No way was he going to just assume she was fine.

Not after a crash like that one.

She could have been killed.

Every instinct warned this was a direct result of their digging into his sister's disappearance.

Someone did not want them getting any closer.

Marshall Medical Center North
8000 AL-69
Guntersville, Alabama, 1:00 p.m.

CHARLY WAS NOT happy with having spent so much time in the ER. To set her worries at ease and because it was the right thing to do, while she suffered through the various procedures for ensuring she had no nonvisible injuries, Billie had gone back to her vehicle and lugged her purchases up to his SUV. The task would have taken far longer but a deputy came along and spotted the trouble. He'd helped Billie with the biggest part of the load, all the while asking questions about the accident. Once the transfer was finished, the deputy had headed to the hospital to talk to Charly. Billie had hurried to her cabin and unloaded the goods, refrigerating all that required that step. The rest sat around her small kitchen.

He'd gotten back to the hospital in time to await the visit from the doctor before she was released and to hopefully ease her frustration.

"Did the fruit seem okay?" She searched his eyes, hers overly concerned about something that didn't matter in the larger scheme of things. "The bananas bruise so easily."

"The bananas and everything else are fine." He smiled. Decided to tease her a little. "A case of water may have flattened the boxes of chocolate."

"Oh no." She made a sad face. "That's the best part of the fruit baskets."

He laughed. "I'm kidding. Everything was fine. You couldn't have packed it better for an accident if you'd planned it."

She nodded. Seemingly satisfied. The nurse had allowed her to put her clothes back on instead of waiting in that less than comfortable gown she'd had to put on at first.

"That deputy who helped you," she said, "came by and took a report. Not much good it will do. The guy was wearing that baseball cap, the bill pulled low so I couldn't see his face. All I know is that he was driving a black SUV." She shook her head. "He didn't hit me, just scared the heck out of me. Maybe he was just some guy in a hurry. I guess the accident was my own fault."

Billie didn't see it that way. "If that pothole hadn't sent you spiraling out of control, I feel confident he would have made another move. Think about it. He drove away and left you in that ditch. If he'd been some guy just driving along, surely he would have stopped or at least called the police."

Regular people didn't leave someone possibly injured stranded in a ditch.

"Makes sense," she agreed. "I forgot to ask. Did the sheriff have any news?"

"He wasn't impressed with my suggestion about the potential pattern over the past sixteen years in his jurisdiction. I can't believe he hadn't already noticed but who knows?" He decided to leave out the part about the sheriff's suggestion that Billie stand down and let him do his job.

"Deputy Lathan talked to me at the market." She rolled her eyes, signaling it wasn't exactly informative or constructive. "They have all sorts of ideas about the trouble you may be causing by nosing around in the investigation and making the locals look bad."

He smiled. "Yeah. I got that impression from Sheriff Malone."

She sighed. "I just wish we would get some sort of news. A sighting. Something. Surely, calls are coming in to that hotline the sheriff's department set up."

"So far, nothing they're telling us about. He told me this morning they're running Briana's and Martin's photos on all the local channels as well as in a statewide bulletin. Sounds like he's taking all the usual protocols. An FBI agent from the Huntsville field office is meeting with him this afternoon."

"Are you going?" She searched his gaze, hope in hers.

"No. Malone didn't invite me and I didn't push. I want him to believe I have complete faith in his ability to get the job done. Besides, my people will hear about the results anyway."

"Deputy Lathan didn't sound as if he or the sheriff trusted what you and your agency are up to." She made a face. "They really hate that we're looking into what happened. But what do they expect? She's your sister for God's sake."

"Sometimes it's best to leave that layer intact," Billie explained. "The one that allows the other side to believe what they choose. But that doesn't mean you're doing what they think you're doing."

Charly nodded, then frowned. She rubbed at the side of her head. "I think I hit the window."

Worry tugged at Billie. He reached up, touched the place above her ear that she had rubbed. "Did they do a scan to make sure there was no injury?"

"They did. I guess we'll know when the doctor shows up."

A soft knock and then the door opened.

Billie glanced at her. "Looks like that's now."

"Afternoon, Ms. Nix." Chart in hand, a man entered the room and walked up to the exam table where Charly sat. "Let's have a look at you, shall we?"

The doctor was maybe forty. Had the suntan of a man who spent plenty of time outdoors. He looked fit. Seemed affable.

"I'm fine, really," she said for about the fifth time. "I bumped my head on the window, and the airbag gave me quite a punch." She put a hand to her chest. "But otherwise I'm fine."

When the doctor had completed a quick exam, he said, "Your scan showed no issues. Other than being sore for a few days I think you're one lucky lady." He stepped back, signaling that he was finished with his exam. "If you start having any issues, persistent headaches, nausea, anything out of the ordinary, go straight to your primary physician or come on back here. Otherwise, I expect you shouldn't see anything more than some bruising from the airbag. Unless you're having significant pain, any over-the-counter pain medication should take care of your needs."

"Thank you." Charly smiled. "I have those at home."

Billie gave the man a nod. When he'd gone, he turned to Charly. "As soon as the nurse comes back with your release papers, we can go."

Charly eased off the table but remained standing close so she could lean against it. "I should call a towing company." She groaned. "I'll need a rental."

"The deputy who helped me move your groceries said he'd call one."

"Good." She blew out a breath. "I guess that only leaves filing my insurance claim."

Her tone warned she was not looking forward to that part. No one ever did. "We missed lunch. Maybe we should stop by JJ's again. Grab some burgers and fries."

"Sure."

She didn't sound overly enthusiastic but that was understandable. Her vehicle was wrecked. She had come close to serious injury herself. Not a good morning.

Billie was just glad she was okay. He thought of his sister and Martin. He sure hoped they were okay, too.

Bradly Retreat
Deep Woods Trail, 2:15 p.m.

CHARLY PAUSED AT her kitchen doorway and surveyed the numerous bags. "This is going to take some time."

"Tell me what to do," Billie offered as he joined her. "I can help."

"There's a pantry over there." She pointed to another smaller doorway. "You can just put things wherever they fit on the shelves. I can organize later. I usually stack the cases of water in there as well."

"On it." He headed across the room.

"I'll separate out the stuff I need to take to the cabins and start on the fruit baskets."

Billie grabbed the first case of water. "You want me to put one of these in Lola? I assume you're stocking water at the cabins, too."

"Yes. Thanks."

He stacked three cases in the pantry and exited the back door with the other. Lola sat only a few yards from the back deck steps. He dropped the case of water into the bed of the UTV and turned to head back inside.

A white pickup coming up the drive from the main road gave him pause. Maybe one of the deputies but not an official vehicle. He waited until the vehicle grew closer then he spotted the Vince's Equipment Rental signage on the door. The pickup parked next to his SUV. A man, late thirties, tall, dark hair, headed toward the front porch.

Billie returned to the kitchen through the back door.

"You have company," he said about the same time a knock sounded at the front door.

Charly stopped sorting fruit. "Anyone you recognize?"

Billie shook his head. "Whoever he is, he's driving a white pickup. Tall guy with dark hair. Vince's Equipment Rental is on the door."

Charly nodded. "Vince Cox." She headed for the front door. "He probably heard about the accident. Word travels fast around here."

As soon as she opened the door, Vince stepped inside and gave her a hug. "What the heck, Charly?" He drew back. "I just heard about your accident. You okay?"

She nodded. "Sure, I'm fine. Come on in." She moved away from the door; the man who clearly had a thing for her followed.

Billie pushed away from the kitchen door and crossed the room. "Billie Jagger." He extended his hand. "Thanks again for allowing us to have a look at your security camera footage."

Vince gave Billie's hand a firm, quick shake. "Happy to help any way I can. It's a shame these things happen."

"It is," Billie agreed.

Vince turned his attention back to Charly. "You know I've got that little Maverick pickup if you need a vehicle to use until yours is prepared. I'm more than happy to bring it over."

Charly looked from him to Billie and back. "I… I suppose that would be a good plan. Save the trouble of getting a rental." She winced. "But I'm not sure how long my SUV will be out of commission, and I have guests coming on Friday."

Vince held up his hands. "I'll have it over here by the time we close. Use it as long as you need to."

"Thanks." Charly smiled, which seemed to make the guy inordinately happy. "I really appreciate it."

He gave her a nod. "I'd better get back to the office. Just wanted to check in with you. You let me know if you need anything at all." He sent a nod in Billie's direction and then was gone.

When Charly closed the door, Billie shot her a grin. "That's some fan you've got there."

Charly waved him off. "He was friends with my husband. He's just being neighborly."

Billie followed her back to the kitchen. The man may have been friends with her husband but what he wanted now was to be friends—good friends—with her.

"Unless I can help you in some way," he said, kicking the idea aside, "I have a call I need to make to a source."

"I'm good here. You do what you need. Finding Briana and Martin is top priority. I don't want to slow you down in any way."

"I'll be back shortly. I want to help." *You*, he didn't

add. His protective instincts were swarming…but other feelings were stirring as well.

You're going way too fast here, pal.

Sometimes a stressful situation caused a person to reach out for any available form of comfort. He didn't want Charly to be his comfort…not like this.

He paused at the door and glanced back at her. But he wanted her…more than was smart for either of them.

Chapter Nine

Bradly Retreat
Deep Woods Trail, 2:30 p.m.

When the door closed behind Billie, Charly relaxed. She'd put on a brave face when he arrived to rescue her. She closed her eyes and shook her head. And he had rescued her. No question about that.

She could have called the police or Vince, for that matter. Even Shelly. But her first thought had been Billie. It was so foolish. They barely knew each other. But she felt drawn to him. Trusted him. On some level she understood that it was about the situation. The tension and fear of having two people—her guests, his family—missing.

But it wasn't just Briana and Martin niggling at her so fiercely. It was all the other blond-haired, blue-eyed women who had gone missing over the past sixteen years. Eight. *Eight!* How did that happen and no one seemed to notice? Had it started with Francesca Andrews? If so, then it was nine! How could that be?

Her father had worked the case. She'd been found wandering along the highway with no memory of where she had been for the past forty-eight hours. The very next day she was taken back to Nashville by her family.

Except then, hardly more than weeks later, she had disappeared again. This time for good.

A new thought occurred to Charly. Her knees felt weak, causing her to lower into a nearby chair. Was it possible that the person or persons who abducted Francesca Andrews were responsible for all the others over the past sixteen years? Could those same people have murdered Charly's parents? No, that couldn't be right.

Could it?

She was going way too far with this random theory. Still, she intended to talk to Billie. Get his thoughts on the matter. It was very possible that her subconscious was infusing the need to solve that part of her past into an unlikely situation that simply shared nothing more than timing.

Charly stood. First, she would complete the guest baskets. They were the final part of prepping the cabins for new guests. By then, Billie would be finished with his calls. They could talk about her new concern then. If it was nothing more than wishful thinking, then at least she went the distance.

She set back to the task of arranging the fruit, along with the box of chocolates, in each basket. The baskets were old, but sometimes vintage was a good thing. They were well made and showed the love of time. Her mother had selected the baskets. They'd been hanging on one of the overhead timbers in the kitchen for years. Charly had known she had to use them. She wouldn't think of changing, even now.

Despite her best efforts to focus her thoughts on the task in front of her, her mind churned with questions. This sinking feeling that she and Billie were on to something terrible with this blond-haired-blue-eyed scenario kept nagging at her. It was a struggle but somehow she managed to finish the last basket.

Seven cabins were rented starting this Friday. She surveyed the seven baskets. They looked good. Surprisingly so considering her level of distraction. One by one she carried each out to Lola. Once they were secured she climbed behind the wheel.

"Mind if I join you?"

She jumped, pressed her hand to her throat. "I didn't hear you walk up."

He slid into the passenger seat. "Sorry. I was so caught up watching you I forgot to speak up and let you know I was here."

She frowned at him. "Watching me?" She laughed. Tucked a stray strand of hair behind her ear. "I look a fright. I'm still a little unsteady after what happened so I'm moving a little slow and a whole lot uncoordinated."

"You," he said as she reached to start the engine, "are an interesting woman to watch. You take such care with whatever you do. Briana is like that. It shows me that you, like my sister, love all that you do."

She shifted into Low and headed for the first cabin. "Well, thank you. I do love this place and being a host to all sorts of people who visit Guntersville. It feels important in some maybe not so important way."

"It is important." He hesitated as she braked at her destination. "Most people work hard and when they take a vacation, it's important they feel they got their money's worth. Equally important is the need to feel the pleasure of it."

She couldn't argue his points. In fact, she thought, glancing at him, he made damned good points.

"I finally received the list of places Martin's credit card was used since they left Chicago."

His tone suggested it wasn't as helpful as he'd hoped. "Anything useful?"

"After they left the airport in Huntsville they drove straight to Guntersville. If they stopped anywhere they used cash. But they did stop at a local restaurant. The Top of the River. Do you know it?"

She nodded. "I do. It's a nice place on the waterfront. Great reputation and great food." She shut off the engine. "Did they come straight here after that?"

"No credit card usage after that so I'm guessing they did." He stood at the back of the vehicle while she reached for a fruit basket. "What items should I take inside?"

Charly pointed to an empty basket she kept hanging on the bar across the top of the backseat. "Put six bottles of water and six each of the snacks in that basket." Shelly had taken care of everything else but Charly had been out of bottled water and snack bars until her ill-fated trip this morning.

Billie took the basket from its hook. "Got it."

She headed to the front door and unlocked it. This cabin, the Woodland she'd named it, had all sorts of fairy decor, including little doors at the bases of many trees. Statues of fairies. The place was actually designed in honor of her sister, Jen. She had loved all things faery when she was a little girl and even well into her teens. She'd left all that stuff when she headed to college. Once Jen was married and Charly had the retreat started, she had used all those knickknacks for this cabin. She'd added lots more as well. It was quite magical with little lights that came on after dark. Orbs hidden in the bushes glowed and twinkled in the enchanting setting.

Billie was coming through the door by the time she had the fruit basket perched on the small dining table.

"How did you come up with all the themes?" he asked.

Charly took the basket he carried and headed to the counter on the kitchen side of the space. As artfully as possible, she arranged the snacks and bottled water. "This one was inspired by my sister's room when we were growing up." She turned to him when she'd emptied the basket. "Each one has a similar story. Someone or something sparked the idea. It started with this one actually and I just kept going until they all had a bit of uniqueness about them."

"You've done a great job."

His compliment warmed her. Made her breath hitch a little. "Thanks." She headed for the door; he followed. "Any other credit card use found?" she asked, moving back to the very important reason he was here.

He closed the door behind them. She handed him the key and he locked it. "On Saturday, they did some shopping downtown on Gunter Avenue. They made purchases in two shops. Had lunch at a café. Then there's the order delivered on Saturday evening."

"Nothing for Sunday?" She had really, really hoped they would learn something about how the couple spent Sunday.

"There was one," he said as they loaded into Lola. "They stopped at a convenience store for gas and snacks on Sunday afternoon."

Charly headed for the next cabin. "And that's it?"

He nodded. "But that's important," he countered, "because five of the eight other victims who match the profile of our pattern visited that same convenience store, too."

She didn't have to be a cop to understand the significance of that information. She didn't even ask how he found this information. The Colby Agency had its sources and they were extensive. "We need to go there. See if the store has cameras."

"They do," Billie told her. "The footage was shared with the police on all five occasions, but nothing came of it according to the case files."

She didn't ask how he knew this, either. "Okay." Her hopes deflated a little. "I guess they didn't find anything relevant to the other cases."

"The question is," he offered as they ferried along to the next destination, "were they looking for the right relevant thing?"

She glanced at him as she navigated the narrow gravel road. "Like anyone who might have been watching the soon-to-be-missing person?"

"Yes. Considering all the women in this town at any given time during tourist season, the person behind these abductions unquestionably picks out the victim and watches her or them until she or they are taken. If there was no pattern, that might not be the case. The specificity of the victims makes all the difference. It changes everything."

Charly parked at the next cabin. "But it's too late to see the footage from those five victims, right? It's probably been erased by now."

"No doubt." He climbed out once more. "Since it was deemed irrelevant it may not have been added to any of the case files. But what we can do is find out if someone who worked at the convenience store during the time those five were taken might be relevant. Or maybe one of them will remember something."

"That person could even be the kidnapper," Charly offered.

"Possibly."

"I say—" Charly grabbed the next fruit basket "—we go there as soon as we finish here." She bit her lip. Hoped she didn't sound too bossy. He might want to go now and get started. Restocking the cabins with snacks, water and fruit baskets was her job, not his. Besides, he certainly didn't need her tagging along.

"That's the plan," he confirmed. "Same thing here?" He jerked his head toward the cabin.

"Same at all of them." Unless a guest asked for specific snacks, they all received the same ones. Some folks had allergies, which necessitated different products. So far, no one had complained either way. She did try to change things up every so often. One of her favorite pastimes was to cruise the net for ideas on how to keep things fresh and memorable around here.

She followed Billie to the door. Having him as a helper made the work seem a lot less like work and more like… Not going there.

Keep your head on straight, Charly. This isn't the time.

Last Chance Shop
Highway 79, 4:00 p.m.

CHARLY SAT IN the passenger seat of Billie's rented SUV. They had been watching the convenience store for about ten minutes. The two employees on duty, one being the owner, had been fairly busy when they first arrived. But now the crowd had dissipated. Her pulse raced with anticipation. She sure hoped they would learn something that helped find Briana and Martin alive and well. Every hour that passed made that end less likely.

"Let's go in," Billie announced.

As they rounded the hood and headed for the entrance, he added, "The same owner has run the place since it opened forty years ago."

"Ned Bates," she said. Charly knew the man. He lived in one of the mansions on the water. He'd built this place to capitalize on the fact that it would be the only gas station between Guntersville and Scottsboro—the last chance to stop for whatever needed. Or maybe the last chance before entering the busier area of Guntersville. At any rate, that was no longer true now.

"He's the older man behind the counter?" Billie asked.

"That's him. Even though he lives in a multimillion-dollar house he still works his forty hours." At least that was what folks said about him. Charly hadn't stopped here in ages, but she had seen him in town from time to time. He was one of many who had offered any help needed to her and Jen when their parents were murdered.

"Sounds like a lot of house for a convenience store owner," Billie suggested.

Charly had never thought about it really, but he was right. "I suppose he may have other investments." Surely, a convenience store didn't provide that level of income. Then again, every time she filled up her gas tank she felt confident someone was getting rich.

"None that I could find," Billie said as he reached for the door.

She couldn't imagine Ned Bates in a trafficking ring but then, she supposed everyone was a suspect until cleared. From Billie's perspective anyway.

As they pushed through the door, a chime announcing someone had entered the store echoed above the soft music. Unlike many convenience stores that blasted rock or some other genre of music, Mr. Bates had the softer, more classic style playing in the background. The second employee on duty had started checking stock on shelves while the owner remained behind the counter, currently looking at his cell phone.

The store was cleaner than the average shop of its kind and sold everything from baby wipes to beer and most things in between.

When they reached the counter, Mr. Bates looked up as if he hadn't heard the signal that someone had entered.

"Charly." He smiled broadly. "I haven't seen you in ages. I guess you stay too busy to get out and about often."

"Busy is good," she said. "How's Mrs. Bates and the family?"

The man had a grown daughter who was a nurse in Huntsville. He had a son, too. Charly couldn't remember either of their names, but she did recall that the son was always running off to California in hopes of finding his big break in the acting business—even at forty something. Inevitably, he always ended up back home, was the rumor. Charly really had no idea.

"They are just fantastic. Susan just had our third grandbaby." He beamed. "We couldn't be happier for her."

"That's great."

"Phil is back home after a round of audition calls out in Hollywood." Mr. Bates smiled broadly but it wasn't quite as bright as the one for his daughter.

"One of these days," Charly said just to be kind, "we're going to see him on the big screen." She gestured to the man at her side. "This is my friend Billie Jagger. His sister, Briana, and her husband are the two who went missing earlier this week."

The older man's expression turned somber. "I heard about that. Just awful." He shook his head. "Sometimes I wonder what this world is coming to."

Yeah, so did a lot of people. Charly decided it was best not to go down that path.

"In my research," Billie spoke up, "I've found eight very similar cases over the past sixteen years that have occurred in the Guntersville area. Five of the women who were abducted visited your store before disappearing. I believe you cooperated with the police and shared the video footage."

Ned nodded, his face grave now. "I surely did. I have a daughter of my own. The idea of something like that is more than I can bear. I'm always happy to help in any way possible when bad things happen."

"I'm sure that footage is no longer available," Billie said, "but I—"

"Oh, I still have it," Ned insisted. "I provided a copy of the first one to Sheriff Bradly—your daddy," he said to Charly. "The other four I provided to Sheriff Malone. But I kept a copy of what I gave them. No way was I destroying what could be evidence. You know I watch a lot of those cold-case shows and sometimes evidence can matter even decades later when it didn't matter at the time of the crime."

Smart man. Charly barely resisted the urged to rush around the counter and hug him. "That's great. If we could have a look at it that would be fantastic."

He nodded, slowly at first then more vigorously. "Sure. I always call Sheriff Malone and remind him anytime anyone goes missing, but he never bothers to look again. Giving him grace, I suppose it's irrelevant, but I feel it's important to remind him." He turned to Billie then. "The couple who's missing now was here, too. I called Malone and sent that to him as soon as I heard what happened. He didn't think the time on the recording was relevant, but I did my duty."

"I really appreciate your diligence," Billie said. "It could make all the difference."

"No problem at all. Tina!"

The woman stocking started for the counter. "Yeah?"

"I'll be in the office for a minute if you'd take care of things out here."

"Sure thing."

Ned led the way to his office. There was a short corridor behind the counter that went past an employee bathroom, a lounge and finally to his office. His desk was large and cluttered. A smaller desk to one side held a computer with a large monitor. This was where he paused.

He settled into the chair. "I'll just pull up the file for you and leave you to it."

Charly didn't know Mr. Bates that well but she really appreciated his being so cooperative. She should have expected as much considering how kind he'd been after her parents' deaths.

When he had the file open on the screen, he rolled back the chair and stood. "There you go. Take as much time as you need." He gestured to the ceiling. "I have cameras in here, too, so I'm happy to leave the two of you to it."

Billie thanked him and then Mr. Bates was gone.

Rather than take the seat at the computer, Billie pulled the chair that sat in front of the bigger desk over to the computer station and gestured for her to take it. Charly settled into the upholstered chair. She liked that he wanted to include her. But then she supposed anyone who worked at the Colby Agency would certainly be well mannered and thoughtful. He took the rolling chair.

As he started the first video, he said, "Let me know if you recognize anyone or spot the same character in more than one video."

Charly leaned forward. "Got it."

This was the oldest video—the one from sixteen years ago when Francesca Andrews went missing. Since the time frame that each victim was at the convenience store was known when the video was downloaded and saved, there was no wait to get to the relevant parts. Mr. Bates had only saved in this file the section that mattered. Charly watched the woman go into the store. Billie hit Pause and they both studied the vehicles in the lot and the people moving toward the store and out of the store in the direction of their vehicles.

She didn't recognize anyone.

He started the video again. She watched, her heart beginning to pound, as Francesca wandered through the store and then went to the counter. She paid for her purchase and headed back out to her car. The video ended about five or so seconds after she drove away. No one appeared to follow her.

"Next up," Billie said. He played the one from fourteen years ago.

Charly figured he was saving the video of Briana and Martin for last.

The third and fourth videos were the same as the first and second but Charly didn't notice anyone or any vehicle that she recognized. The last one, the one from three years ago, was up next.

Charly barely remembered this one happening. It was during Alex's final days, and he was all that was on her mind. Her whole world was wrapped up in making him comfortable.

One of the figures on the screen made her frown. "Wait."

Billie hit Pause and turned to her. "You recognize someone?"

The woman who'd been abducted the next night had already gotten into her car, but a lone man was walking toward his own vehicle.

"Do you think we can zoom in closer?"

The man's vehicle was a black truck, which was as common as mosquitoes in the summer around here. The way it was parked didn't allow a view of the license plate. Billie zoomed in closer on the man's face.

Charly straightened. "That's Kerrick Rogers."

"Rogers?" Billie looked to her. "The same Rogers as the owner of the place Francesca Andrews was staying when she disappeared?"

"That's the one." The thumping in Charly's chest got a little faster.

"But you didn't recognize him in any of the others?"

"Let's look again." Anticipation had her on the edge of her seat.

Billie went back to the first video icon and hit Play.

"Wait," she said. He hit Pause and she pointed to the screen. "Is that him?" This was sixteen years ago but the swagger was the same. He would have been in his early twenties. "Play it again."

The video restarted. Charly watched carefully. "The way he moves looks so similar. Can we zoom in?"

Billie zoomed in. The image was grainy but Charly felt sure it was him—Kerrick.

"Let's move on to the next one," she urged, excitement building like a fire in the woods in the dead of summer.

In all four of the videos that followed he was there—at least someone who looked like Kerrick Rogers. Walked like him. In two he wore the same sort of black hoodie.

"All right." Billie glanced at her. "Let's play the newest one."

Charly nodded.

This would be the one with Briana and Martin. Her stomach tightened. She could only imagine how Billie felt.

Billie hit Play and the images on the screen came to life. This was on Sunday before they went missing on Monday night. Last Sunday, she realized. It felt like half a lifetime ago.

Martin got out of the white SUV and was preparing to pump gas. He said something to Briana as she headed into the store. Probably told her some item he wanted.

Charly instinctively reached for Billie's hand, gave it a squeeze. This was his sister. Watching her had to be ripping him apart inside.

Briana wore a white sundress with pink flowers. Her flip-flops were pink, too. Her long blond hair draped around her shoulders. She looked far younger than twenty-nine.

While they watched, Briana went inside and took her time gathering a few items. She took them to the counter and paid. Then she headed for the door, a white plastic bag heavy with her purchases in her free hand. Outside, another vehicle pulled into the lot. Silver truck. A figure emerged from the driver's side and started toward the store entrance. He and Briana passed right by each other.

The bottom dropped out of Charly's stomach.

"That's him."

Kerrick Rogers.

Chapter Ten

Lost in the Woods Getaway
Scottsboro Highway, 5:30 p.m.

Charly braced as Billie turned onto the drive that led to their destination.

The Rogers family had started their getaway only a few years after they were married more than three decades ago. The place wasn't in Guntersville proper, but it was only a few miles from the city limits. Mr. Bates's convenience store lay smack in the middle of that stretch of highway 79 between the Lost in the Woods Getaway and Guntersville.

Unlike Charly's retreat, the place offered more than cabins. There was everything from glass dome dining under the stars to yurts, hot tubs to soaking pools. Laney Rogers organized all sorts of activities and had even in recent years built a spa-like salon offering everything from manicures to massages.

Billie shut off the engine in front of the office, which was a large cabin with a parking area in front. Like Charly, the owner lived in the cabin that also served as an office. But this one was far larger than Charly's. Over the years it had been renovated and expanded into a much more elaborate place. There was nothing elaborate about Charly's cabin or her retreat. Her place offered a more rustic charm.

The office was still open—the sign on the door showed that it closed at six and provided a number to call for after-hours service. Billie opened the door, a bell over it tinkled and Charly entered first. Laney was alone in the office and appeared to be tidying up in preparation for closing. She glanced up, spotted Charly then glanced at Billie. She smiled but it was as fake as the eyelashes she pasted on every morning.

Charly silently chastised herself for thinking such a thing. Laney was a gossip and plenty arrogant, but she was still a somewhat nice person.

Now she was just kidding herself.

"Well, good evening, folks." Laney shifted the smile in Charly's direction and she could have sworn it dimmed. "What brings you out this way?" Her mouth suddenly formed an "O" and her hand went to her chest. "Oh my, Charly, I heard about your accident. I'm so glad you're okay."

Of course she'd heard. Charly summoned a smile of her own. "Thanks."

The entrance door opened, the bell tinkling. Charly glanced back in that direction. Kerrick Rogers, Laney's son and only offspring, swaggered into the office and wouldn't you know he wore a black hoodie. Seemed a little warm for a long-sleeved hoodie to Charly. The man dressed more like a teenager than a nearly forty-year-old.

"Cabin ten is squared away," he said as he approached the counter and plopped the key there. Then he propped against it as if interested in whatever his mom was doing with her surprise visitors.

"Thanks, baby," Laney said, her smile broader than before. She turned to Charly. "Charly, you know my son, Kerrick."

There had been a time—before Alex—when Laney had done all in her power to throw Charly and Kerrick together. Then Charly's retreat could have become the Getaway II. Never in a million years.

Charly glanced at the man who'd tried his best to fulfill his mama's wish. "Sure. We run into each other all the time." They didn't really all that often, but it sounded good. "This is Billie Jagger," Charly went on, looking from Kerrick to his mother. "His sister is Briana Willard. She and her husband are the couple who went missing the other night."

Kerrick's gaze flitted to Billie then back to his mother. His expression remained as placid as when he'd first walked through the door. Totally unlike his mother, who could go from sad and distressed to perky and happy in less than a second.

Laney gasped. "Oh, my Lord. I'm so sorry to hear this, Mr. Jagger. We're all sure praying that they'll be found safe and sound. The whole community is on the lookout for that poor couple. It breaks my heart every time I see it on the news."

"Thank you," Billie said. "I appreciate that." He looked to Kerrick then. "Actually, I came here hoping to speak with you, Kerrick."

Laney's sympathetic expression changed instantly. "That's... Why would you want to speak with Kerrick?"

She divided her attention between her son and Billie. "Do you need some help with something?"

Charly opted to keep her mouth shut since she didn't know how Billie intended to approach the questioning. Besides, she was having far too much fun watching the ever-changing reactions of the woman behind the counter. It wasn't easy to undo the unflappable Laney Rogers. Charly might never see this moment again.

"We just watched the video footage from the last known sighting of my sister," Billie explained. "She was at the Last Chance convenience store. Charly—" he gestured to her "—recognized Kerrick as a person who arrived while Briana and her husband were there."

Laney's face showed absolute horror as she stared at her son.

Kerrick shrugged. "When was that?" he asked, his attention fixed on Billie.

"Sunday afternoon, just after two." Billie watched him closely, analyzing his every tick, every shift in body language.

Charly imagined his intense gaze was unnerving to the other man. She glanced at Laney. His mother was certainly undone.

Kerrick nodded slowly, his gaze narrowed, as if he was trying to recall. "What were they driving?"

"White Ford SUV," Billie said, his gaze still glued to the guy.

"Martin," Charly said, "her husband, was pumping gas. Briana went inside. I'm sure you saw her. Gorgeous blonde, late twenties. You've probably seen her on the news, too. But that afternoon she was wearing a really cute white sundress with pink flowers. And pink flip-flops."

Kerrick nodded again, relaxing visibly now that his attention had shifted to Charly. "Yeah. Yeah. She had a six-pack of my favorite beer."

Charly's insides froze. How had he seen the beer? It was in a bag.

"Did she say anything to you?" Billie asked. "Did you notice if she was upset? Maybe she looked scared?"

"This is getting a little intense," Laney spoke up when her son didn't immediately respond to the new barrage of questions. "Maybe you need to speak with Sheriff Malone about this."

Kerrick held up a hand. "It's all good, Mom." His attention swung back to Billie, his body language going cocky again. "She did now that you mention it. She looked pretty upset. And the way she was glaring in the direction of her husband." He moved his head slowly side to side. "She was fired up about something for sure and it was probably his fault."

Charly looked to Billie to gauge his reaction. He seemed calm and collected except for the tick in his jaw, which was new to her. Obviously, he was angry but holding back in hopes of learning something relevant.

Kerrick laughed. "Just kidding. She didn't seem upset or anything. Just focused on walking to her SUV." Kerrick nodded once and gave a wink. "Her husband is one lucky guy."

Charly's jaw dropped. Was the man an idiot? Any second she expected Billie to go off on him.

Finally, Billie shook his head. "I wish the convenience store had audio." He exhaled a big breath. "Sadly, only video." He tilted his head and studied the older man in the hoodie. "Did you know that Mr. Bates sent copies of the video footage from numerous cases over the years? Starting with Francesca Andrews. You remember her, right?"

All the swagger went right out of the other man's bearing. His expression fell like a rock from a cliff.

Laney abruptly did a one-eighty and hurried into the private office beyond the counter. Billie and Kerrick remained locked in a staring contest. If Charly had her guess, the woman was calling her husband for backup.

Charly needed to say something to break the tension before it expanded any further. "It's really great that he's been diligent that way," she blurted. "It helps the police to know where a person was just before they disappeared. You can gather all sorts of information from where they've been." She shrugged. Scrambled mentally to think of something else while Kerrick eyed her now with blatant suspicion.

"And who they encountered at each location," Billie said.

The features of Kerrick Rogers's face tightened. "Are you trying to accuse me of something? Is that what this is about?"

"Francesca was found," Charly said, her voice a little high-pitched. "Thank God. Too bad she disappeared again from her home in Nashville. Still, I'm sure your mama," she went on as Laney hurried back to the counter, "was glad the worst didn't happen here. It's really a terrifying prospect."

"I've called Sheriff Malone," Laney announced. "He's on his way."

If Kerrick had looked stricken before, he appeared

downright ready to run this time. "Why'd you do that?" He flung one hand toward Billie. "We're just talking. Everyone knows Francesca was staying here. Hell, that's ancient history." His bravado back, he pointed a finger and a narrowed gaze on Billie. "Besides, this guy's just fishing. He's worried about his sister. Ain't that right, friend?"

Billie nodded. "That's right, *friend.* I suppose I got my hopes up a little about you when I saw that in five of the nine cases involving blonde women who've gone missing over the past sixteen years, you were seen at the Last Chance convenience store at the same time they were—only hours or days before they disappeared."

Laney gasped. "If I hadn't already called the sheriff I would throw you out of here right now."

She glanced beyond them to the wide windows that overlooked the glamorous entrance to her retreat in hopes of the sheriff's arrival, or maybe worried someone else might be watching. Charly was certain she would be mortified if any of her guests noticed a confrontation in the office.

"No need to be upset," Charly assured her. "It's a reasonable assessment. I saw the videos myself."

Laney's glower shot toward Charly. "This is a small town. With all the tourists in the summer, folks are bound to be at the same place at the same time. What about it?"

"Not one thing," Billie assured her. "It's only relevant if there were words exchanged or if one person followed the other to and from that location." He stared directly at Kerrick then. "Did you leave around the same time Briana and her husband did from that convenience store?"

"Don't say another word, Kerrick," Laney shouted,

coming around to their side of the counter to stand next to her son. "That's about enough. I understand you're upset, Mr. Jagger. But your implications are unfounded and unwanted. Sheriff Malone investigated every single time that Kerrick was seen on CCTV in those cases. Just because he left at the same time as the woman who went missing doesn't mean he did one thing he shouldn't have. Other people were leaving at that same time, too."

But he hadn't left at the same time as any of the victims in the footage they saw at the Last Chance. Charly's nerve endings started to tingle. Laney was just saying whatever necessary to cover for her son. "I'm sure it doesn't mean anything," she offered.

"Course it doesn't," Laney screeched. "Rob Decker at the Stop and Go and Paul Grant at the Pit all said that Kerrick was a regular at their establishments. It wasn't unusual to see him on their CCTV on any given day. Just because some tourist who disappeared was, too, doesn't mean a thing." She pointed a finger at Charly. "Lenny Reed was on those videos as often as Kerrick was. Why aren't you harassing him?"

Before Kerrick or anyone else could say more, the sheriff's truck parked in front of the office. Laney rushed to the door to meet him. Charly was still trying to figure out what she meant about Rob Decker and Paul Grant.

"Thanks so much, Tully," she said, going for a whisper but failing miserably, "for not coming in sirens and lights blazing."

He gave her a nod and then surveyed the room. "What's this all about?" His gaze landed last on Charly.

"We saw the video footage Ned Bates has on file," Charly explained. "In all five cases where a victim who later went missing visited his store, Kerrick was there at that same time. We just wanted to see if he noticed anything about Briana and Martin. If they were upset or whatever. Or maybe he saw someone paying extra attention to them." She said this part to Kerrick.

His mama shook her head when he would have responded.

Sheriff Malone pushed his cap up and scratched at his forehead. "I realize your daddy was the sheriff for most of your growing up," he offered, "and I recall him taking you along on lots of trips into the field. But that doesn't make you a cop, Charly. There are laws about how this is done."

"I wasn't trying to do your job," she hastened to say.

"She was assisting me," Billie said, moving to her side. "She knows the names and faces here and I don't. I needed her eyes and her knowledge. Because I am an investigator, and I will not stop looking for my sister and her husband until I find them. If that means stepping on toes or hitting nerves… Well then," he said, glancing at Kerrick and his mother then back to the sheriff, "I guess you'll be getting a lot of calls like this."

The sheriff sat his hands on his hips. "I can understand given the situation, but there's a right way to do these things, and coming in here and upsetting this lady and her son is not one of them."

"It's all right, Sheriff," Kerrick urged. "We understand. Don't we, Mama?"

She nodded, though she didn't appear as certain as her son pretended to be.

"Fact is," Sheriff Malone added, "we have reason to believe the person who took your sister and her husband was driving a black SUV based on the security video from Vince Cox, and you said—" he directed at Charly "—that the vehicle that caused you to run off the road was a black SUV."

"I do not drive a black SUV," Kerrick piped up. "I have a silver truck."

Billie gave a nod of acknowledgment. "I appreciate the clarification. But that still leaves me with serious questions about your appearance," he said to Kerrick, "in so many captured moments with the victims over the years."

The sheriff held up a hand. "I think we can all agree that sometimes events are just coincidences."

Billie laughed a dry, quick sound. "I don't believe in coincidence, sir."

Kerrick harrumphed. "Call it bad luck, then. Call it whatever you want. But I had nothing to do with your sister or any of the others you're talking about."

Billie stared him directly in the eye. "Besides my sister and Francesca, how do you know who I'm talking about?"

For one split second Kerrick had that deer-in-the-headlights look on his face, then he snapped out of it. "You said something about nine women." Then he threw up his hands. "I'm out of here. I have work to do."

He walked out of the office, those remaining staring at him.

"I… I can't have this," Laney babbled. "As sorry as I am for your situation, I just can't have these disruptions." She zeroed in on Charly. "Surely, you understand it's bad for business."

"I think," Sheriff Malone said, "the two of you should be on your way. If you have questions about this case or any other in my jurisdiction, you should direct those questions to me. Do not," he warned, "go around upsetting folks with accusations that are wholly unfounded."

"Understood." Billie looked to Charly, and they headed for the exit.

It wasn't until they were in his SUV and driving away that Billie spoke again. "The remarks his mother made about the two other businesses suggests he was captured on other security footage with other victims."

Charly's heart started that frantic pounding. "That's what I was thinking, too. I know Rob Decker and Paul Grant. I believe they'll talk to us."

"Just tell me which way to go," Billie said.

Decker Residence
Riverbend Circle, 6:50 p.m.

Rob Decker's Stop and Go was on Gunter Avenue not far from the Highway 79 intersection. But they didn't go to his gas station; instead, they went to his house. Rob was older than her father would be if he were still alive, late seventies, maybe eighty. She couldn't see him at work at this hour.

The house was one of those modern structures built in the eighties and nineties. This one was showing its age a bit but the view of the channel was quite nice.

After ringing the doorbell, her assumption about the man likely being at home was confirmed when Rob himself answered the door.

"Mr. Decker," Charly said before he could ask who they were and what they wanted, "you may not remember me. I'm Charly, Sheriff Bradly's younger daughter."

Rob's face lit. "Well, of course I remember you! You're the spitting image of your mother."

Charly relaxed. She got that a lot. Jen got their father's much darker coloring. Charly had the lighter brown hair and green eyes of their mother. "I hope we're not interrupting your dinner."

"No! Come on in." He drew the door open wider. "As Carol and I have gotten older, we prefer dinner a little earlier since we end up in bed earlier." He looked from Charly to Billie. "You kids have no idea how lucky you are to be so young."

They followed him into the living room where his wife sat on the sofa watching television. The volume was muted. She glanced up as they walked in. "Just catching the weather." She waved dismissively at the television. "Who wants to hear the news anymore?"

"Nice to see you, Mrs. Decker." Charly didn't know the wife as well, but her father had considered Rob a friend. The welcome reception so far gave her hope the couple would be amenable to answering questions. "This is my friend, Billie Jagger," Charly explained, looking from the wife to the husband. "His sister is Briana Willard. I'm sure you've heard she and her husband are missing."

"It's just awful," Mrs. Decker bemoaned, her hand going to her throat. "Really awful. I'm so sorry," she said, looking in Billie's direction. "Has there been any news?"

"No, ma'am, I'm afraid not."

"Sit down." Rob gestured to the pair of sofas facing each other. "Tell us how we can help."

Charly and Billie settled on the sofa facing Mr. and Mrs. Decker.

"We don't want to take up a lot of your time," Billie said. "We just have a couple of questions."

Rob nodded. "Fire away, Mr. Jagger." He grinned. "Any relation to Mick?"

God, Charly had almost asked that a dozen times no matter that she knew the answer was undoubtedly no; she could barely resist. Now, thanks to Rob, she didn't have to.

"Actually," Billie said, "the answer is no but my mother would tell you that she is certain there is a connection somewhere in my father's family history."

They all shared a laugh that went a long way in lowering the tension for Charly, especially considering the questions they had come to ask.

"Mr. Decker," Billie began, "do you recall sharing footage with the sheriff regarding any of the victims who've gone missing over the past ten or so years?"

The older man's eyes widened. "I do. Anytime I see there's been anything like that happening, I always check my security camera footage for the days surrounding the trouble. It only overwrites every seven days so I can generally find the time frame in question without any trouble. But this couple who's missing now didn't come into my place."

Made sense to Charly that Briana and Martin had used a convenience store on the other side of the bridge since they were staying at Bradly Retreat.

"It's my understanding," Billie went on, "that Kerrick Rogers was at your place of business at the same time as one of the victims."

Rob shook his head. "Oh no, that's not right."

Billie and Charly shared a look.

"It was three of the victims. Ella Franklin back five years ago. Lara Young twelve years ago."

"No, that's wrong, Rob," his wife spoke up. "Lara was thirteen years ago. The one you're thinking of was Michele Colton. She was twelve years ago. But Kerrick was there all three times. You mentioned that to the sheriff, but he didn't seem to think it was relevant."

Charly mentally ticked off the names of the nine they knew about. Francesca Andrews, Tina Dayton, Peyton North, Lara Young, Michele Colton, Ella Franklin, Janet Miller, Hilary Trenton. And Briana Willard. All blond-haired white females with blue eyes. As well as three male boyfriends or husbands, including Martin.

All these missing people with unresolved cases had been captured on video at the same stop as Kerrick Rogers. Maybe it was coincidence as he wanted them to believe. But Charly didn't believe it for a second and she knew for certain Billie didn't, either. This was wrong and the sheriff was ignoring it!

It took every ounce of strength Charly had to keep this to herself.

"You don't happen to still have copies of the videos?" Billie asked.

Charly didn't breathe until his question was answered.

"No. As I said, I turned copies over to Malone in each instance and then I just let the system overwrite itself after that. But those three visits, once each, were the only times those girls came into my place during their stay in Guntersville."

"Do you remember anything specific about any of those three occurrences?" Charly asked. "Any trouble or behavior that caught your eye while they were in your store?"

"Well," Rob said, "not really. Not that I can recall anyway."

"You did say," Mrs. Decker reminded him, "that one boy watched every move the Franklin girl made."

Rob nodded. "That's true but she was a looker and any man still breathing would have been looking."

Mrs. Decker shook her head. "Men," she muttered.

"Was that Kerrick Rogers?" Billie asked.

"No," Rob said. "That was Lenny Reed. He was practically foaming at the mouth watching Ella Franklin like a mad dog about to pounce on a victim."

Lenny Reed. The man Laney Rogers had mentioned.

"Lenny does that to all the girls," Mrs. Decker said. "That boy was a mess. But that new wife of his has straightened him out pretty good. He goes to church every Sunday now."

A new wife and church every Sunday didn't rule him out in Charly's book.

"I can't believe the sheriff hasn't found anything." Rob shook his head. "It's just like the others. It's as if they vanish into thin air with no evidence left behind."

"It's hard to believe it can keep happening over and over," Charly mentioned.

"It is," Rob said. He looked to Billie. "My question is when are we going to have better methods in a case like this? There has to be a way."

"No question," Billie agreed, then he passed Mr. Decker one of his cards. "Please call me if you or Mrs. Decker think of anything at all you believe might help me in my search for Briana and her husband."

"Count on it," Mr. Decker assured him.

On the way to the door the two said again how sorry they were and how their thoughts and prayers would be with Billie and his family.

Charly suddenly wondered about Billie's family. The Willards', too. They must be devastated as well. She could only imagine how his parents felt.

When they were in his SUV, she forced her mind to move on to the necessary business and said, "Next stop is the home of Paul Grant, lifelong bachelor and revered pit master."

"Just tell me where to turn."

Grant Residence
Val Monte Drive, 7:50 p.m.

PAUL GRANT LIVED in a first-floor condo right on the lake. Unlike Rob's place, this one was very new. Very contemporary and quite expensive. His home was mere yards from the water and very near popular restaurants as well as his own, the Pit—a renowned barbecue restaurant.

Paul was a good man. When her parents were murdered, he'd brought prepared meals to her and Jen for weeks. When Jen had gone back to college, Paul had checked on Charly regularly. Anytime she needed to cater an activity for her guests, Paul always came through with great food and a good deal. He was like an uncle. And he'd loved Alex. They'd spent many Saturday afternoons on the water fishing. And when Alex died, Paul had been there for her all over again. He was kind and generous.

Billie rang the doorbell.

Almost immediately, the man's voice came to them via the speaker in his video doorbell. "May I help you?"

"Hey, Mr. Grant. It's Charly. I hope we're not interrupting your evening."

"Charly!" Five seconds later the door opened. He looked from Charly to Billie and back. "Come on in here. It's been too long."

"I know. I'm sorry. Life gets in the way." Charly followed him inside, Billie close behind her.

He gave her a hug. "How have you been doing?"

"I'm good," she said. "Staying busy with the cabins."

"Good. Staying busy is the best route for moving on." He looked to Billie.

"This is Billie Jagger," she explained. "His sister, Briana, and her husband were staying at my place when they disappeared. I'm sure you've seen the news. Sheriff Malone held a press conference about them."

"I have." He clapped Billie on the arm. "I was so sorry to hear about that. Damn, it's a crazy world anymore."

"Thank you. We're doing all we can to find them."

Paul's eyebrows hiked up as he shifted his attention back to Charly. "Malone not doing his job right? Not the way your father did, I'll wager."

Charly smiled. "He'd have a difficult time ever being as good as my father."

"You are correct," Paul agreed. "Have a seat." He indicated the equally contemporary sectional sofa and chairs.

"We can't stay long," Charly explained. She could smell the man's dinner probably waiting in the oven for him. "We just wanted to know about any security footage from the Pit that may have captured one or more of the victims who've gone missing over the years. It was mentioned to me that you had provided input to the investigations."

"I have. Rob Decker, too," he said.

"We spoke to Mr. Decker," Billie told him. "He was very helpful."

Paul nodded. "Well, this was two years ago. Miss Hilary Trenton dropped by to have dinner at my restaurant. She was alone. I remember her well because she made it a point to leave a great review on Google that very night. A few days later when I saw she was missing, I was very disturbed. That's when I called the sheriff and sent along a copy of the video from that night. Of course, I didn't expect it to provide anything in the way of evidence, but I hoped it would help fill in any blanks in the timeline." He laughed. "I may have watched too much crime TV."

"What you did is a very important step," Billie assured him. "Never doubt that."

"I do what I can." Paul nodded. "It's the least any of us can do."

"Did Hilary seem okay? Not upset or anything?" Charly asked.

"She seemed fine." He frowned. "There was this one fellow who sort of followed her to her car when she was leaving. Lenny Reed." Paul shook his head. "The guy leered at her. But I've never known Lenny to be any trouble. Still, the young lady didn't know that. It was obvious she was very uncomfortable."

"Was there anyone else that caught your eye in the video?" Billie asked.

"Well, Kerrick Rogers. He shoved Lenny and told him to stop acting crazy. Hilary seemed grateful for his help as she got into her car and left. Both Kerrick and

Lenny left right after her—separately, of course. When I spoke to Sheriff Malone about it, I asked him to speak to Lenny about his behavior. I hope he did."

"Thank you, Mr. Grant." Billie passed him a card. "Please call me if you think of anything else that might help us find my sister and her husband."

"I surely will. If there's anything you need," he offered, "or if there's some way I can help, please let me know."

Paul showed them to the door. He gave Charly another hug and urged her not to be a stranger.

When they were driving away she couldn't help noticing how quiet Billie was. The worry was getting to him. Of course it was. His sister and her husband had been missing for three days with no word, no evidence, nothing.

"I wish there were something I could say." Her voice sounded loud after a minute or so of silence. "I know this is incredibly difficult and it doesn't seem to be getting any easier. It's like searching for a needle in a haystack. We keep coming up with more of the same."

When he braked for a traffic light, he turned to her. "It is and I'm grateful to have you on my team. I genuinely appreciate what you're doing, Charly. I hope you know that. The people we've interviewed likely wouldn't have spoken to me at all without you."

She smiled. "I'm glad and I do know. I'll help as long as you need me to."

His smile warmed her. Made her wish again there was more she could do. Some new tactic that would make all the difference. Surely, someone had seen something. All that person had to do was come forward—even anonymously. She'd watched a replay of the press conference the sheriff held and he'd urged the community to do just that.

The rest of the trip home was made in silence.

A truck sat next to her cabin. At first, she thought someone was waiting but then she remembered Vince said he would bring that extra truck of his for her to use.

She should be glad, but she hated accepting any of his overtures for fear of giving him the wrong idea.

Charly and Billie climbed out of the SUV at the same time and headed for her porch. She was suddenly starving and totally exhausted. Her body ached from the crash. She reached the door first but paused. There was a folded paper stuck in the crack between the door and the frame. Had she missed a delivery or a potential guest? No one had called her cell. She pulled the paper loose and unfolded it. Words. Typewritten.

Looking into the past is a bad idea. Remember what happened to your parents.

Shock radiated through her. What the heck? There were no other markings on the single page. Who would send her a warning like this? She shook her head and handed the notc to Billie.

More importantly, why would anyone do this?

Chapter Eleven

Bradly Retreat
Deep Woods Trail, 9:20 p.m.

Billie located the ingredients for making a salad in the fridge. He'd put most of them away during the transfer of goods from her crashed vehicle so he was aware the needed fixings were handy. Charly sat at the table staring at the note as if reading it over and over or analyzing it forward and back as well as from all angles would tell her who had left the warning on her door. But he understood how that felt so he didn't urge her not to… It was impossible. When it came to something like this, the mind had a will of its own.

She suddenly pushed back her chair and stood, swayed just a little. Obviously, she was tired. Shaken. Sadly, he couldn't fix that, either.

"I should be doing that," she insisted. "You're my guest."

They had gone over this once before. She worried that it was his sister who was missing, and that he should sit while she figured out dinner. She had even offered to order something to be delivered. Each time he had ushered her back into her chair and told her the same thing he was going to tell her now. "It's better if I'm focused on a task."

It was true. The moment he stopped doing something—anything—his mind dragged out the hellish thoughts about his sister and just how bad the trouble she was in might be. Dozens of questions about who had taken her and why. Sheer terror that she and Martin were human trafficking victims who, like many others, would never be found or would be horribly abused and injured before being rescued.

He couldn't endure those thoughts. He gave himself a mental shake to dispel the nightmare snatching at the edges of his mind. It was better to stay busy.

He'd checked his email and there was nothing new from his resources at the agency.

For now, there was little else anyone could do except keep digging for a lead. Not an easy thing to do with his little sister missing. He kept remembering the wedding and how happy she had looked. Martin had been beaming as well. The man was deeply in love with Briana. She'd made him wait long enough. Billie smiled to himself as he diced a tomato.

"What're you smiling about?"

Charly's voice drew him back to the present. He set the knife aside, tossed the tomato cubes onto the two plates where the lettuce waited.

"I was thinking about how happy Briana looked on her wedding day."

Charly pushed in her chair and went to the fridge, withdrew a bottle of salad dressing and a container of turkey slices. "I'll bet she looked really beautiful," she suggested. "Martin must have been counting his blessings."

Billie laughed. "I know he was. When Briana left for college she swore that no matter what, she was not getting married until she was too old to care about dating anymore." He picked up a cucumber and started slicing it. "An age she deemed to be about thirty, which she will turn on her next birthday."

Charly laughed. "She sounds like a girl who knew what she wanted right from the beginning—to be in charge of her own destiny."

"She was that for sure—still is," Billie agreed, pride swelling in his chest. "When Martin asked the big question, she immediately launched into the conditions he needed to agree to before she answered."

Charly rounded up a bag of croutons. "Did she share her conditions with you or your family?"

"She did. She spelled it all out at Sunday dinner the day after his proposal." The cucumber slices went on the salads next. He paused to look directly at Charly. "No children until she was at least thirty-five. No careers taking over their lives—especially after they had children. He had to kiss her and tell her he loved her every morning before they went their separate ways. They could never speak by phone without ending the conversation with *I love you*. No matter how many years of marriage passed." He held up a hand. "Oh yeah, and they could never part or go to sleep angry at each other."

"Those are good conditions." Charly nodded. "All married couples should follow those rules."

Yeah, Billie felt the same way. It was far too easy to allow life to get in the way of enjoying those you loved.

"What about you and Alex?" He opened the container

of turkey and prepared a few slices for the salads. "Did you have rules like those?"

"We did, sort of. We never laid them out the way Briana did, but it was sort of an unspoken guide. My parents were firm believers in not allowing the sun to go down on your anger—like in the Bible. My parents were an excellent example of what a good marriage looks like."

Billie considered what he should ask next. He didn't want to wade too deeply into sensitive territory but there were things he felt they should talk about. "What happened to your parents," he began, shook his head, "there was never any real closure for you and your sister."

The words came out more a statement than a question. Her expression shifted instantly to something distant and sad, no matter that sixteen years had passed. When did a person fully get over something like that? Maybe never.

"It was assumed that the shooter was someone my father had brought to justice at some point in his career—probably more recently than in the distant past. Probably not the perp himself but a friend or family member who actually did the deed." She reached into a cupboard and withdrew two glasses. "The investigation appeared to be thorough. I followed interim sheriff at the time Tully Malone's work closely. Whether it was to appease a devastated daughter or because he actually cared, he kept me up to speed pretty closely."

She said all this in a monotone that told him this was her practiced answer.

"But they never found any evidence. Not even a shell casing at the scene."

"Nothing. It was fast and clean. I can only assume," she went on, "that someone pretended to need assistance.

Maybe a flat tire or some other car trouble. My dad would have pulled over to help and they were shot where they sat in the vehicle. The coroner estimated they had been shot approximately an hour before someone came along and found them."

Damn. That was enough for now. "Since we haven't been digging around in your parents' case," he offered, "I'm assuming that warning you received is about Francesca Andrews and the others."

Charly chewed on her lower lip. The move had him thinking about things he shouldn't have on his mind at a time like this. His sister was missing…her new husband was as well. And this woman was sticking her neck out, possibly making enemies with people she had known her whole life in order to help him.

She needed protecting, too…from him and what he'd come here to do.

"I guess so," Charly agreed. "My parents' case hasn't been looked at in years. It's not like Jen and I have forgotten but there comes a time when you have to accept certain things, and not being able to find their killer was one we had to come to terms with or go crazy beating our heads against a wall." She hissed out a breath. Shook her head. "I know how that sounds but for the first five or six years I spent endless hours making calls and bugging Sheriff Malone. My sister and I hired private investigators. We did everything we knew to do and found nothing. So we finally let it go. We had to. But we didn't give up or forget about them. We just made the decision to move on with our lives."

He reached out, squeezed her arm. "I completely understand. The two of you did the right thing. Your parents would have wanted you to get on with your lives. I'm sure you both realize this. No matter how painful an event is, there has to come a point when you move beyond it enough to keep on living yourself."

She nodded. "You're right. They wouldn't have wanted us to live in the past. But I will never forget and I will never give up on finding something so I do a little research now and then. Whenever there is a case anywhere near here that has similarities to theirs, I look into it. I follow the social media pages of several people who went to prison because of my father." She shrugged. "I watch and I listen. Right now, that's the best I can do."

"I'll say it again," he said, smiling, "you missed your calling, Charly Nix."

She did a little eye roll. "You want tea or water? Or coke? I'm fresh out of beer."

"How about some of that sweet tea you Southerners love so much?"

"Hey." She reached into the fridge. "We all have our vices."

Salads and glasses of tea on the table, they settled and dug in. For a while they ate without talking. It had been a long day. Billie thought about that note and tried piecing it into the puzzle he was putting together about Briana's and Martin's disappearances. The note was clearly a warning about digging into the other missing women, which meant that the note was connected…somehow to Briana and Martin. There was no other conclusion to reach.

"The way I see it," Charly said after finishing off half her salad, "only one of a very small number of people could have left that warning."

"Kerrick Rogers," he suggested.

"Or his mother," Charly countered. "Sheriff Malone. The only other people we discussed the subject with are Rob Decker and Paul Grant. We'd just left Paul's home and driven straight here so I don't think he would have had time to be the one. I can't see Rob having any reason to be involved."

"Kerrick could have called whoever he works with—assuming he's involved with the disappearances," Billie suggested. "That person may have left the note."

Charly nodded. "That's a possibility. I don't think he would be the primary person running any sort of operation involving…"

She didn't say the rest but they both recognized what they were talking about.

"Human trafficking," Billie said the words that had been twisting in his gut since he heard the news. "That's what we're looking at here. The ones like the nine we've looked at are special orders for specific customers."

"The blond hair and blue eyes, pale skin," Charly said, her tone showing her distaste at the prospect. "That's how you found a pattern."

"Right." Billie pushed the remainder of his salad aside. Talking about this and eating just didn't work. "There are all sorts of requests, as you can imagine. From coloring to age. Height and weight. Even education and employment."

Charly squeezed her eyes shut and shook her head. "What kind of person does this?" She held up a hand. "I know, I just mean it's unfathomable to me."

"It's horrific." The thought of Briana being snatched

and sold like some sort of retail item ripped his insides like a knife thrusting and then twisting in his gut.

Charly pressed a hand to her throat. “I’m sorry. I haven’t even asked how your parents are doing. I’m sure they’re beside themselves. And Martin’s parents.”

Billie scrubbed a hand over his jaw. “There hasn’t really been a good time,” he pointed out. The two of them hadn’t talked about his family until now. When he’d first arrived, sharing information with a stranger was the last thing he’d wanted to do, but Charly wasn’t a stranger anymore.

“True,” she agreed.

“For my family,” he explained, “this is the worst time something like this could happen. Our father is dying. He has MS. His condition started to deteriorate even more rapidly earlier this year, which was why Briana pushed up her wedding date from September to July. She wanted him to be there. We all did. With his condition continuing to deteriorate so rapidly, Mother can’t leave him. Otherwise, she would be here.”

“I am so sorry.” Charly pressed her fingers to her lips for a moment. “This truly is a nightmare on multiple levels for you and your family.”

He tried to smile, failed. “It hasn’t been a good year for sure— other than Briana’s wedding.”

Charly squared her shoulders. “We have to find them.” Something like outrage bloomed on her face. “Tomorrow,” she declared, “we are going to follow Kerrick Rogers until we catch him alone and we’re going to—”

“Talk to him,” Billie interjected.

She gave a little shrug. “Knowing Kerrick it might take a little extra incentive.”

Billie laughed. "I'm sure you mean like the offer of money."

She blinked. "Well, yeah, sure." She laughed then. "No, that is not what I mean. I mean…" She shook her head. "Sorry. My father would be ashamed of me suggesting that we torture the truth out of the guy."

Billie cut her some slack. "Don't think I haven't toyed with the idea." He would love to beat the hell out of whoever was responsible for Briana's and Martin's abductions.

"That makes me feel less like a bad person," she admitted. "But I can't promise I won't punch Kerrick if he even hints at the idea he had anything to do with this."

"You'll have to get in line," Billie assured her.

They laughed together and for that one split second, Billie felt an instant of relief.

Silence lingered for a bit, then he remembered her other question. "As for Martin's parents, they are hanging in there. They wanted to rush down here but I talked them out of it. They're older and the stress is bad enough without being here."

"Good point." She sighed. "I remember how horrible it was after…my parents. The hoping and praying…"

Another stretch of silence. She picked at the salad she had abandoned. He watched her. There was something about the curve of her cheek…the shape of her lips. Funny how he thought of that with all that was happening. But she was different than anyone he'd ever met and he couldn't help himself.

She glanced up. "If there's something you want to ask, just ask."

He didn't think she was ready to hear what had been on his mind in that moment, so he moved on to something relevant. "At any time when you were looking into your parents' murders, did any person—the sheriff, anyone—ever try to warn you off? Did you receive any threats or warnings like the one we found tonight?"

"No. Never. I had a good many people offer ideas on what happened but nothing that panned out."

Billie sipped the tea. Cool, sweet, what wasn't to like? "Can you give me a couple of examples?"

"The Russians," she said. "Mr. Hodges, a World War II veteran, suggested my father had been a spy and had to be stopped because he'd learned something he wasn't supposed to know."

Billie had to hand it to her; that was one he hadn't expected. "Certainly an interesting theory."

"His family said he was never the same after the war. When my parents were murdered he was well into eighty and suffering from dementia. I just listened to whatever he had to say," Charly explained. "I didn't want to hurt his feelings."

Billie imagined her sixteen years younger dealing with all that having a family member—much less two—murdered entailed. He also decided then and there that she was the stronger of the two sisters no matter that Jen was the older one. Charly was brave and damned smart.

"I'm sure his family appreciated your patience."

"They did. His older daughter, the one who took care of him, lives in one of the houses on the end of Bakers Chapel near the church. Mr. Hodges used to walk from one end of the road to the other every day. He was surprisingly energetic for his age. Sadly that was also the death of him. He was hit by a driver who left the scene.

He wouldn't have survived the injuries, but I don't know how the driver just rushed away rather than calling for help. His daughter said she had worried that would happen but there was no containing him other than locking him in a room, and she didn't want to do that."

"Some people are cowards," Billie said. "Only a coward would leave an elderly man dying on the side of the road rather than call for help." The idea made Billie ill.

"Definitely a coward," Charly agreed. "Another anonymous tip about my parents was that the killer was a former deputy my father had fired. Sheriff Malone investigated that one, but the man accused had an airtight alibi." She shook her head. "Another one insisted it was a former lover of my mother's, which was preposterous. Particularly since the supposed lover was Sheriff Malone." She laughed. "My mama was not a fan of the man. She was certain he took every opportunity to undermine my father. Not to mention he was a lot younger than her."

Billie chose not to point out that because her mother was older or had shown her dislike for Malone didn't mean she hadn't been involved with him. It was always easier to hate on a former lover. No reason to upset her by suggesting as much. There was also no reason to believe the murders of Charly's parents had anything to do with Briana's and Martin's disappearances. Yet, anyway.

Charly shook her head. "I just know it had to be Kerrick who left that note."

The discussion about her parents had obviously grown too painful or uncomfortable to continue. He hadn't meant to go back into the subject just now, but the truth was that talking about her parents' case was far easier than analyzing his sister's.

"He would do something like that," she went on. "And another thing—" she looked directly at Billie then "—how did he know Briana had bought the same beer he liked? He couldn't have seen the beer clearly in that bag. And since he wasn't in the store when she picked it out and paid for it, he had to have seen it after that."

"You're right." Billie had already come to that conclusion, but he was restraining the urge to pounce on that one detail. "One of the things I've learned from the brilliant attorneys the agency employs is that when being questioned by the police or anyone else relevant to a case, never say more than necessary. Never offer information that could incriminate you. Kerrick Rogers incriminated himself. Either because he let his mouth override his brain or just because he wanted to sound like he knew more than we did. Whatever the case, it bears further investigation."

"Do you think he's realized his mistake?" Charly pushed her chair back, stood, picked up her plate and carried it to the trash can to empty it.

Billie followed and did the same. "If he's smart it has crossed his mind." They walked together to the sink.

As she rinsed her plate and fork, her gaze narrowed. "Maybe he sent the note to distract us from focusing on his slip of the tongue."

Billie rinsed his plate, barely holding back a grin. "That would be my assessment."

She stacked the plates and forks but left them in the sink and dried her hands. "I'm not sure I can wait until morning. I think we need to go question him right now."

Billie shrugged. "Let him stew. If we're right, by morning he'll be even more out of sorts after worrying overnight."

"Okay." She set her hands on her hips. "What do we do, then?"

Loaded question. He exiled the thought. "Let's talk about who else may have left that note."

"It was him," she countered. "Had to be."

"But what if it wasn't him?" Billie challenged. "What if it was the guy who was your husband's friend and who would like to be more than a friend to you?"

She made a face. "Vince?"

"He brought you that truck to use." The guy definitely wanted her attention.

"Why would he get involved?" Her frown deepened. "He was only about twenty-two or -three when my parents were murdered."

"People kill at far younger ages," he reminded her.

"But I don't think Vince is the killer type," she argued. "I don't think he's ever even had a parking ticket."

His head went back in an aha gesture. "So you like him, too."

"No." She scowled. "I mean, sure I like him as a neighbor. Maybe even a friend. But I do not like him like *that*. Never. I can't be around him without thinking about Alex."

"Why not?" Billie hadn't meant to ask the question. In fact, he hadn't intended to start down this path, damn it. Who she liked was none of his business and was completely irrelevant to why he was here. But he hadn't been able to resist. She made him want to spar with her. Made him want to kiss her actually…but that would not be a smart move just now.

He desperately needed her help… He could not risk alienating her on any level.

"The truth is," she said pointedly, hands still on her hips, "I haven't wanted to like anyone else that way. Not since I met Alex. I was eighteen years old then. He was my everything and then he was gone." She drew in a big breath. "Actually, I had begun to think that part of me had gone out of business for good."

Now he felt like a total ass for starting this thing. "I'm—"

"But," she interrupted, "lately I've had these feelings that were so foreign to me that I almost didn't recognize them."

Before he could respond, she grabbed him by the face with her hands, drew him down to her level and kissed him hard.

He pulled her into his arms and deepened the kiss. Despite the nightmare of all that had happened and despite his misgivings, he relaxed against her soft body. Lost himself to the feel of her lips on his.

But then he stopped. Drew back. He wasn't using her to distract himself and although he felt this need for her was more…he wasn't taking the risk.

"We should slow this down and maybe get some sleep." He tried hard not to sound so breathless but that hadn't worked. *She* made him breathless…made him want her more by just looking at him the way she was at the moment.

"You're right. We should call it a night."

But rather than show him to the door, she led him to

her bedroom. He didn't resist. Instead, he slowly undressed her while she undressed him. He kissed his way down her throat. Picked her up and carried her to the bed. Her arms and legs went around him and the rest of the world disappeared.

Chapter Twelve

Friday, July 10

Bradly Retreat
Deep Woods Trail, 7:30 a.m.

Charly was immensely grateful that Billie was gone when she woke up. Not that she regretted last night. No way. She tossed aside the dryer she'd used on her hair and hugged herself. She had a right at this point to have a moment. To feel something again. Alex had been gone for three years. As surprising as it was…as much as she had expected the morning after to be filled with utter and total guilt, she felt none.

What she felt was regret that she'd lost a wonderful husband. A part of him would always be with her.

Billie had been correct when he'd said that Alex would want her to move on. Who could say whether one year or three was the proper length of time to grieve? But Charly trusted herself on that one. Last night had felt very right. And pretty damned amazing. Even if she had been the one to push him over the line when he'd resisted.

She brushed her hair and then twisted it into a long braid. It was far too wild to leave loose when she had work to do. Shelly was coming to hang around the office and to check in the new arrivals. Billie hadn't said for sure what he intended to do or where he planned to start this morning. Talk had not been on their minds after dinner last night. She decided he hadn't gone far, since his SUV was still parked out front next to the borrowed truck. Technically, she hadn't borrowed it. Vince had insisted on leaving it. But she supposed that was a good thing. If Billie had places to go that didn't include her, she would need some means of transportation and Lola was not road worthy because she lacked seat belts.

Billie had probably returned to his cabin to shower and change. His clothes and toiletries were there. Maybe he had a conference call with his agency or with the sheriff. Whatever the case, he would fill her in when he came back.

She tidied the bedcovers, inhaling the scent of him and their time together. A smile spread across her lips. She knew better than to get used to having him around. As soon as he found Briana and Martin, he would be going back to Chicago. His work was there…his family was there.

A trickle of new regret slid through her. She had known Billie barely three days and already she felt like they were old friends. She hadn't sensed such a connection to another person since Alex.

"Let it go, Charly," she murmured.

In the kitchen she scrambled a few eggs and prepared some toast. Prepping and cooking an easy breakfast prevented her from dwelling on things she could not change. Just as the two slices of browned bread popped out of the toaster, a knock followed by "Good morning" echoed through the house.

Billie entered the kitchen. He glanced at the eggs she'd

scraped onto two plates and smiled. "If that extra plate is for me I will gladly do the cleanup." He sent her an unreadable look. "Or whatever you need."

Feeling flushed at the idea of what those words meant, she placed a slice of toast on each plate. "Grab those and I'll get the orange juice."

He carried the plates to the table. She met him there with two glasses and the orange juice. Once they'd settled, Charly felt a little shy sitting across from him knowing that he'd seen every part of her. Then again, she smiled to herself, she had seen and explored every part of him as well. No need to be embarrassed or shy. Easier said than done. But then she was out of practice on these things.

She took a breath and asked, "So do you do this often?"

It wasn't until she asked the question that she realized how it sounded. Dear God. She closed her eyes for a second in frustration at her bad choice in words.

"Have eggs and toast with a beautiful woman?" His lips spread into a sexy grin. "Or spend the night in her bed?"

She fought the urge to rush from the room but she couldn't stop the need to shift around in her seat. "Yes… no." She shook her head. "I mean yes to the last part."

He laughed. "No. I do not do this often. In fact, becoming personally involved with a client is frowned upon. Usually, the client is the one who's suffered some tragedy or been haunted by some person or the past. I would never take advantage of anyone in a vulnerable situation."

"I'm not a client," she responded far too quickly. "And I'm not in a vulnerable spot."

"No. You are not." He pushed the eggs around on the plate with his fork. "But I have my doubts as to whether that would have mattered this time." His gaze locked with hers and she could feel the heat across the table. "I recognize my limitations, and resisting you may have been beyond my ability."

She managed a single nod, certain her cheeks were red. "Good."

"Good," he agreed.

"Are we going to track down Kerrick today?" she asked before tearing off a bite of toast. Changing the subject was the only way she could stop squirming in her seat. She also felt confident that getting on with business would help keep her foot out of her mouth.

"If we can find him away from his mother, I think that is a great starting place." He sipped his orange juice.

Charly chewed her lip. There was one way that might work. "I could call him. Tell him I need to talk to him alone. I think he might be willing to do that."

Billie's gaze narrowed. "Has he indicated that he's interested in you?"

She shrugged. "He's interested in any female still breathing, I think." Okay, that was unkind. "Years ago his mother tried to push us together. But that was a long time ago. More recently, he has asked me to dinner a couple of times. To a local ball game once. But I've always said no. I suppose that suggests he is to some degree."

"He's not your type?" Billie finished off his toast.

"I don't really know him. I see him in town occasionally but that's it. We've never really been friends. He was a couple of years ahead of me in school. I suppose we're really no more than acquaintances. I'm far more familiar with his mother and I don't think he could ever be my type because she's his mother."

She winced. "Sorry. That really was mean."

"It was just the truth." Billie studied her a moment. "Does he have a group of friends he hangs out with?"

Charly had to think about that question. "There are a couple of guys I've seen him with from time to time. Arlon Jones. He has a bait and tackle store on the waterfront. His daddy started it decades ago and Arlon took over when he retired." She searched her memory for the others. "Finn Grayson," she said, recalling another. "He's a boat mechanic." She scrunched her face in concentration once more. "Well, I don't know that he actually does the work anymore. His business has boomed over the years. His shop services boats for just about everybody around here. Especially the folks who have private docks and mega mansions."

Billie downed the last of his orange juice. "Anyone else?"

Who was that other guy? Oh yeah. She remembered now. "Perry Hillard. He's just..." How did she describe Perry? "He's like the junk guy. He's always picking up stuff people put out to the road for trash collection. You know, old tables or chairs or damaged bicycles. Basically anything and everything. You can even call him and have him come by and remove junk you don't want or need anymore. Not the sort of stuff you can donate to someone who might need it, but the damaged or nonworking stuff that no one wants."

"Let's start with the junk guy." He tilted his head toward the counter. "I'm cleaning up."

Charly took her plate to the sink. "You'll get no argument from me."

While he was on dishwashing duty, Shelly arrived. Charly joined her at the desk in the corner of the living room she used as an office. She gave her the rundown on who was checking in and which cabins they had selected. The one the Willards had used was still off-limits. And the treehouse, of course.

"So that's the PI?" Shelly whispered, stealing a glance toward the kitchen.

Charly nodded. "That's him."

"Wow." She waggled her eyebrows. "All I can say is he's hot."

Charly waved her off. "I'll have my cell with me if you need to reach me."

Billie appeared at the door. "You ready?"

She was. Absolutely. Charly grabbed her shoulder bag and draped it across her. She rarely carried her bag unless she was headed into town for supplies, but she had no idea what this day would call for.

"I am," she announced.

When they were in his SUV she gave him the directions to the last known address she had for Perry. It was a small, wooded lot next to an RV park off the beaten path.

Hillard Residence
Cha-La-Kee Road, 9:00 a.m.

PERRY HILLARD'S SMALL travel trailer sat in the woods a good distance from the road. A little farther down that same road was the RV campground perched on the edge of the river. In addition to numerous other amenities, the location was also recognized for its view of the well-known home with the built-in lighthouse.

But Perry's little tin box on wheels that served as his home was only known for being the kind of place you didn't go after dark. All around the property was the junk he "collected." Charly had heard the rumors that his so-called collecting was merely a cover for selling drugs. She couldn't say if there was any truth to the rumor. The one time she'd hired Perry to haul away some old appliances was when she'd updated those in her cabin. Alex had suggested she not hire him again. He'd been suspicious of the guy and Alex generally liked everyone. She had apparently exiled Perry to the far regions of her memory along with so many other Alex-related moments far too painful to remember.

Perry's rusty blue pickup—the same one he drove when he picked up her appliances—sat next to the little trailer that was a similar color of faded blue.

When Billie parked and shut off the engine, he turned to her. "Let me approach the door first. If he's here and I don't see any issues, you can join me."

"That's his truck so he's probably home," she said first, but then she argued, "But he doesn't know you. You should let me go in first. I can call out his name. Tell him who I am. He'll recognize me."

"Not a good idea," Billie countered. "I should go first."

As if to defy both their conclusions, two large and admittedly vicious-looking dogs trotted from behind the little dingy blue trailer and bounded toward the SUV.

"You were saying," Charly teased.

As fearless as she was, she did not mess with unfamiliar dogs. Particularly those who looked like guard dogs. Aggressive guard dogs owned by someone of questionable standing. And it wasn't that she didn't like dogs. She loved dogs. She and Alex had adored Watson—their big old black Lab. Alex had given the puppy to her the same night he proposed. Watson had been with them their entire marriage until he died in his sleep three days after Alex. Watson had been old, almost thirteen, and he'd been declining for a while. But he'd hung in there until Alex was gone and then it was like he allowed himself to let go.

Another devastating moment for Charly. She'd loved that damned dog. And like her inability to feel anything in the way of interest in another intimate relationship, she hadn't been able to bear the idea of another dog. There was no way to replace that sweet, loyal animal.

"I'm good with dogs," Billie offered with a glance in her direction.

She laughed. "Famous last words." She reached in front of him and pressed the horn. The dogs started to howl and circle the SUV.

Billie looked from her to the trailer and back. "I guess we'll know in a minute if he's home."

"We will." She pressed the horn again; this time she held it down for a second or two longer.

The front door opened, and a shirtless, low-slung-jean-clad Perry Hillard stumbled out, almost face-planting in the overgrown grass. Even from thirty feet away there was no missing the scowl on his face.

He patted his right thigh and whistled. The two animals went to him immediately.

She and Billie exchanged a glance.

He opened his door and Charly did the same. From the corner of her eye she saw the worried look he cast her way. The idea that he felt compelled to protect her was sweet but not really necessary. She could take care of herself—except maybe when she ended up in a ditch.

"Perry!" she shouted as she moved toward the front of the SUV. "We didn't wake you, did we?" She supposed it was early for some folks.

The dogs whined but stayed at his side, their bodies quivering with tension. They wanted to protect their master and his home.

"What you up to, Charly girl?" He muttered something to the dogs and they visibly relaxed.

She and Billie continued slowly walking toward the man. Long, thick hair he'd fastened into a ponytail at the nape of his neck looked mussed and ready to fall from its tie. He'd probably slept with it that way. He was too skinny and average height. A scar on his left jaw elicited second looks from strangers but reminded those who knew him that his old man had been a bad, bad person who beat his kid way too often. When Perry decided to fight back—with a knife—his daddy had taken it away from him and given him something to remember his mistake by. The scar.

Strange she hadn't remembered that until she was standing in front of the man.

"I'm looking for Kerrick," she told him, not exactly a lie. She and Billie hadn't discussed how they intended to approach this guy. She was just making it up as she went along. "He was supposed to get back to me on some questions we had for him."

That part was totally a lie.

Perry ignored her comment and looked at Billie for the first time. "Who's your friend?"

"Billie Jagger," he said, extending his hand as he drew within range of exchanging that sort of pleasantry with the guy.

Perry's chin went up as he offered a fist bump instead of a shake. "Oh yeah, the PI from Chicago."

Word got around fast. No surprise. For all its tourists and weekenders, Guntersville was basically a small town with a tight community of year-round residents.

Billie obliged him with a fist bump. "My sister and brother-in-law are the couple who were kidnapped on Monday night. Charly is helping me with my search to find out what happened and to find them. Did you happen to run into either of them? Or maybe hear anything about them? Any help you can provide would be greatly appreciated."

He made a face, shook his head. "Nah. I didn't see 'em. Kerrick did," he offered. "That guy sees everything. You talk to him already?" This he directed at Charly.

She'd already told him she was looking for Kerrick. He was either fishing to see if her story would hold up or he was seriously hungover and couldn't remember squat.

"I did. Last night. He said he ran into them at the Last Chance the other night. He was supposed to check with you and Finn to see if either of you saw them, but he didn't get back to me." If Charly was lucky he wouldn't realize there really hadn't been time between last night and this morning. "I guess he didn't talk to you yet."

Perry grunted. "You know Kerrick. If it ain't about him, it ain't important."

Charly laughed. "Yeah, I guess you're right."

Perry raised an eyebrow at her. "He still trying to get you to go out with him?"

Why did guys always ask that? Charly shook her head. "The man finally got it that I wasn't interested."

"Well, that's too bad for him." Perry looked her up and down. "You ever get bored, you call me."

"I'll remember that," Charly lied, again.

"It's too bad," Billie said, "that you didn't see my sister and her husband. There's a big reward. Did you hear about that?"

He had Perry's full attention now. "Reward? I didn't see nothing about a reward on the news."

"Ten thousand dollars," Billie said. "I'm only offering it to people I believe can help us find Briana and Martin. If you're one of those people—" he withdrew a business card and passed it to the other man "—call me when you have something to share."

"Yeah." He looked from the card to Billie. "I'll do that. Ask around and whatnot."

"Thanks, Perry," Charly said. "We're really worried about them. We need all the help we can get. Whoever finds them will be a hero and a whole lot richer."

A smile tugged at his mouth. "Yeah. That's right. You like heroes?"

Charly worked up a smile. "What woman doesn't?"

"Let me hear from you soon," Billie said.

Perry gave him a nod, and they turned to walk back to the SUV.

Charly held her breath, hoping against hope the dogs didn't suddenly rush them.

"Hey, man," Perry shouted.

Charly froze.

Billie turned around. Charly followed his move.

"You any relation to the Rolling Stones lead man?"

Billie laughed. "Not to my knowledge."

"Too bad, man, he's a badass."

Charly waited to do an about-face when Billie did. They walked to the SUV, climbed in and headed back to the road. "Good move offering the reward. Perry will be spreading the news all over town."

"I just hope he decides he'd rather have the money than to keep a secret."

Charly turned fully toward him, studied his profile. "You believe he knows something?"

"He didn't ask any questions about the situation," Billie pointed out as he navigated the SUV back toward town.

"Which possibly means he already knew all there was to know."

"That was the impression I got." Billie braked for an intersection. "Most people would be curious about the details. He wasn't curious at all, which tells me he already knows something."

"Wow." Charly leaned more deeply into her seat. "That makes total sense." She turned to Billie again. "I'll bet as soon as we left he made a call to Kerrick to find out why he didn't mention talking to us."

"Or," Billie suggested, "why he didn't mention there was a reward."

"Kerrick will be furious that we didn't tell him." She was starting to like this investigator gig more and more.

"And," Billie went on, "he'll wonder if we didn't because we believe he's involved. If my read on Hillard is accurate, his buddy Kerrick will be worried that ten thousand dollars might buy his friend's loyalty."

"I get it. You're creating friction in the ranks. Prompting action from the players."

"Exactly." He flashed her a grin that made her heart beat faster. "Now we go on to the next friend of Kerrick Rogers and then the next one after that until his concern for keeping his secrets is more than he can contain."

"He'll do something and that will…" She shrugged. "Maybe give us information we don't have now."

"It will certainly confirm our suspicions about Rogers. He'll inform whoever is over him in the network and that will cause a reaction."

Made total sense. The simplicity of it had her anxious for the next step.

"As much as I dislike Kerrick," Charly admitted, "I wouldn't have believed he would do something like this."

"If our suspicions are correct," Billie explained, "Rogers may have been involved in this sort of thing for a long time. Maybe longer than we know. But my impression at this point is that he's a low-level player. We need him to prompt someone higher up. That's how we find Briana and Martin."

Charly hoped that happened soon. The longer the couple was missing… Well, she didn't have to imagine the rest. She knew what would happen.

The Boat Fixer
AL-79, 10:15 a.m.

FINN GRAYSON HAD three employees and not one of them knew where he was. But all three agreed that he'd left only five or so minutes before they arrived and no one had any idea where he'd gone.

Billie left his card and a request that Finn call him as soon as possible regarding the missing couple. He went to great lengths to include as much information as possible, including the hefty reward. All eyes had been on him when he and Charly walked out of the repair shop.

"What now?" she asked as she climbed back into the passenger seat.

"Now we drive back by Hillard's place and see if he has a visitor."

"You think he called Finn and they're having an emergency meeting." Charly's pulse sped up. They could be getting close.

"It's possible and we have nothing but a few minutes' time to lose by checking."

Charly could hardly breathe as he retraced the route to the Cha-La-Kee Road. Since the trailer and Hillard's driveway weren't close to the road, Billie would drive slowly past the turnoff while Charly peered down the narrow road. She wasn't sure what kind of vehicle Finn drove but if she saw anything besides the rusty old blue truck, Billie was turning around and pulling into that driveway.

She held her breath as they drove past.

A small red truck was parked right next to the blue one.

"Someone is there," Charly blurted. She turned to Billie as he slowed to make a turn in the middle of the road. "There's a red truck parked next to Perry's."

"Let's see who this visitor is and if it's who we think it is, then we'll know we're on to something."

They needed a break. They really, really did.

And this could be it!

Chapter Thirteen

Hillard Residence
Cha-La-Kee Road, 11:00 a.m.

Billie turned onto the driveway of Perry Hillard's property. "Stay low," he said to Charly. "Just in case."

She wasn't sure what he expected might happen but clearly he was concerned. Shootouts and all manner of attacks whizzed through her head. "All right." She eased down a little in the seat but not so far that she couldn't see.

Perry sauntered out of the house, his two dogs running past him. He set his hands on his hips and stared at the SUV they were in. At least he'd put on a T-shirt and they were no longer forced to see his countable ribs. The man needed to eat.

Before Charly could ask what next, Billie opened his door and got out.

Her heart thumped against her sternum.

The dogs rocketed toward him.

"Easy now," he said softly.

Charly shoved her door open in hopes of distracting them.

It worked. The dogs rushed to her side of the SUV. Maybe not a great move.

Her heart rocketed into her throat as she held stone still.

Perry called out a command that sounded indistinguishable to Charly, but to her relief the dogs alerted and then without hesitation bounded toward him.

Since Billie was already at the front of the SUV, likely headed in her direction, she joined him there.

"Not a good move," he said in an aside to her.

"Yeah, well, it worked, didn't it?" she whispered in his direction.

"Did you forget something?" Perry asked as he took his time strolling in their direction as if he didn't want them to get too close to his trailer.

Still no sign of the other vehicle's driver. She had no idea if it belonged to Finn.

"We were looking for Finn," Charly spoke up.

"We were told he was here," Billie added as he hitched his head toward the red truck. "That's his truck, isn't it?"

Perry stared at Charly for a long moment, then he gave Billie the same. "Finn," he shouted over his shoulder.

The other man poked his head out the door. "Yeah?"

"Charly and her friend want to talk to you," Perry called back, not turning in that direction as if he worried about giving his back to them.

With obvious reluctance, Finn Grayson stepped out the door and slammed it shut. He poked his hands into the pockets of his jeans and walked their way. He wore a tee that sported the logo of his business. Like Perry, he had long hair but his was stick straight and hung loose around his shoulders.

When he arrived at his friend's side, he said, "What's up?" He looked from Charly to Billie in expectation.

Since his gaze lingered on Billie, Charly stayed quiet.

"I'm looking for my sister, Briana," Billie said. "She and her husband went missing Monday night. I was given a handful of names of people who might have the right connections to find information. Yours was one of them."

"I know nothing about your sister and her husband," he said without hesitation. "I never saw them around and barely even heard they were missing." He glanced at his friend. "Perry here told me a couple days ago. That was the first I'd heard of it."

"There's a reward," Perry said quietly, the words obviously meant for Finn's ears.

"Ten thousand dollars," Charly spoke up. "I'm sure you know plenty of people who could use ten thousand dollars."

"The payment would be in cash," Billie said, backing her up.

Perry and Finn shared a look. "Too bad we don't know anything," Finn said.

"That is too bad," Billie agreed. "But if you know anyone who might know something, that could count, too."

"Kerrick sounded like he might have some information," Charly offered, pushing the point with a total lie. But Billie had said they were looking for reactions. Hoping to prompt actions.

"Then maybe you should talk to him again," Finn countered. "I'd love to get my hands on ten k, but I'm not in the loop. Not even near it."

"We've been looking for him," Charly went on with

another fib. "His mama probably has him running errands today."

This prompted snickers from the two men. "Yeah," Perry said. "He's a mama's boy all right. His mama tells him when to take a piss."

"What loop did you mean?" Billie asked, ignoring the other comments.

Both men stared at him.

"You said—" he looked to Finn "—that you weren't in the *loop*."

Finn exaggerated a shrug. "I just mean whoever is working on the case, I'm not in the know."

"You have friends in the sheriff's department?" Billie fired back.

Finn grew still, dangerously still. "I have friends in all kinds of places." There was no humor in his tone or his expression now. "Friends who look out for me."

Billie made a confused sound. He turned to Charly. "Did Kerrick mention protecting either one of these guys?"

Charly shook her head slowly side to side. "He didn't mention protecting anyone but himself."

The two stared at each other again. "You tried to call him, right?" Perry asked Finn.

"Yeah. He didn't answer."

"I guess we're not the only people he's avoiding since he said more than he should have last night," Charly said to Billie. "I suppose we could give what we have to your contact at the FBI." She shrugged. "Then you can just keep the reward."

"Guess so," Billie agreed. He turned back to the two men. "Thanks for your help."

They had just reached the SUV when Finn called out to them. Rather than remain standing next to Perry, he jogged to catch up with them.

"Was there something else?" Billie asked.

Charly glanced at Perry, who was on his cell phone. He appeared to be scrolling or sending a message. Her heart started that impatient thumping again. They were definitely on to something here. As much as she would prefer to believe that no one in this town—especially anyone she knew—would do such a thing as to kidnap a person. To use or sell that person. This felt exactly like the sort of business these two were covering up. She shuddered at the idea.

"If," Finn said, keeping his voice down, "I could find some info that would help, could I give it to you without anyone knowing my identity. People get upset when you share their business."

"Sure," Billie agreed. "I always protect my sources."

Finn glanced back at Perry. "I'll talk to my friend. See what we can find out. We know people who deal in all sorts of bad stuff. Not that we do." He pressed a hand to his chest. "But there are those we're acquainted with who do."

"Why haven't you gone to Sheriff Malone?" Charly demanded, more firmly than she'd intended.

Finn's gaze narrowed on her. "Because I don't trust him. Anyone who knows him doesn't trust him." He eyed Charly. "Didn't your daddy ever tell you about him?"

The impact of his words shook her. "I'm not sure what you mean?" She wasn't about to put words in his mouth.

"Well," Finn said, his posture and tone going cocky,

"I'll bet if your folks could talk to you from the grave they'd tell you to beware of that particular badge."

Outrage with no shortage of razor-sharp pain flew through her. "What're you suggesting?"

"Ask the sheriff yourself," he dared. "Why do you think their case has never been solved?"

"Finn!" Perry shouted.

He glanced at his friend, who had remained near the trailer. "What?" The single word was drenched in annoyance.

"We have to go."

He looked to Charly then to Billie. "Be safe out there. You never know where the trouble is going to come from."

They loaded back up in Billie's SUV and drove away. As he turned onto the road, Charly asked, "What now?" She was still reeling with what Finn had said about her parents. The man couldn't know this. He was just trying to get under her skin. Or confuse her.

Mission accomplished.

"We'll find a place to park where we won't be easily spotted and then we'll see what they do next."

She drew in a deep breath. "With the way we rattled them, they won't be able to keep all this to themselves."

She decided not to mention how badly she had been rattled.

"They will not." Billie backed into a small turnoff that went nowhere except into the woods and then ended as abruptly as it began.

The position gave them a narrow view—between two trees—of where the Hillard driveway connected with the road. Charly twisted in her seat and set her gaze on that gap between the trees.

Silence filled the passenger compartment for a while, then Billie said, "You can't be sure what he said about your parents has any merit. He may have only been trying to prod a reaction from you. To shake you."

"I know." She didn't glance at him. She was too determined to keep her eyes on that spot. "I've always felt Sheriff Malone could have done a better job of finding the truth, but I have no proof. Those two PIs didn't find anything either so I don't know."

"But," Billie said softly, "that doesn't mean it can't be found."

A smile nudged at her lips. He was right. Even in one's darkest hour there was always hope and possibility.

TEN MINUTES PASSED before there was movement. The red truck pulled out onto Cha-La-Kee Road heading away from where Charly and Billie were parked.

"There they go," she warned him.

Billie waited long enough for her nerves to be jumping before he followed.

Charly didn't realize she was sitting forward until they stopped at a traffic light on Gunter Avenue. The red truck was at the next light ahead of them. So far the two didn't appear to realize they were being followed. The lights changed at almost the same time. Both vehicles pulled forward.

This was the first time Charly could remember ever wanting to chew her fingernails.

When the pair made the turn that would take them in

the opposite direction, then kept driving until they were outside Guntersville City limits, she glanced at Billie. "They could be driving to the Getaway."

"The Rogerses' place?" he asked.

"That would be my guess, but they could be going somewhere else. I can't be sure."

"I guess we'll find out."

Ten minutes later the truck turned into the drive to the Lost in the Woods Getaway. Billie drove past the driveway and found another spot to park where they could watch the comings and goings from that destination.

"Are there any buildings or cabins farther back that are not part of the Rogerses' property? Maybe another road on the back side of these woods?"

"I've never really done any exploring on that property, but I know there's a road back there. It runs parallel with the back side of the Rogerses' property."

"We'll wait and see what our guys in the truck do. See if Kerrick makes an appearance and then we'll check out that road."

If Kerrick was somehow involved in all this, was he just the guy who picked out targets? Did he actually get his hands dirty by taking victims? Charly was pretty sure it hadn't been him driving that SUV in the video from the night Briana and Martin disappeared. Maybe he was the babysitter? The guy who watched over the ones taken until they were moved to the next step? Was that even a thing?

If it was, then it was possible Kerrick had some place where he kept his victims until they were moved on or picked up. She'd watched a couple of movies about human trafficking that were based on true stories. She was well aware that no community was exempt from such terrible things. But it just didn't seem possible that someone she had known her entire life would be that sort of monster.

But all those people who did such bad things had families. Mothers. Father. Siblings…friends.

She was being naive. Mostly because she didn't want to believe a guy not much older than her, who had grown up here, would do such a horrible thing.

Money.

It was all about money just like the drug business. Her father had warned her and Jen that as long as there was a demand for bad things, there would always be bad people doing those bad things.

Money was a powerful motivator.

Running an operation like hers and the one the Rogers family operated was not for the faint of heart. There were lean years. In the beginning there were a lot of expenses that were no longer an issue. But upkeep sometimes made a year barely profitable. Alex had said if they survived the first three years they would be okay, and if they survived five years they were good to go, barring any unforeseen catastrophes.

Like having not one but two guests go missing.

Charly exiled the thought. She glanced at the man sitting patiently behind the steering wheel. She would gladly watch her business decline if it meant he found his sister and her new husband. Their lives were far more important than any other aspect of all this.

The prospect of the two becoming just another statistic was too painful to consider. She could only imagine how Billie and the families felt.

She studied his profile and decided to try to lighten the moment. "You know you do look a little like him—Mick Jagger, I mean—back in his younger days when he was actually kind of hot."

Billie shifted his attention to her. "I know we are not having this conversation."

She laughed. "I'll bet you got that all the time in high school."

A grin hitched up one side of his mouth. "From time to time."

Charly relaxed in her seat. "Tell me about Briana." She knew a little about the younger woman but not so much that was deep or personal.

"She was the biggest pain in the butt when she was a kid." He laughed. "She was always after me to help her to do this or include her on that. Especially when I had friends over."

He fell silent for a moment.

"But I love her. Loved her then. Love her now. She was one of the best parts of growing up. An amazing sister." He looked at Charly. "I was always her hero. At least until she grew up and turned into this superwoman who believes she can do anything without the help of her big brother. She's one of the strongest women I know."

"She won't make this easy for them." Charly wouldn't, either, and sometimes that sort of strength could be an issue with surviving.

"She will not," he agreed. "She's smart, too. I wouldn't put it past her to find a way to escape." He tapped his temple. "She has this way of dissecting an issue and finding a way to fix it or go around it. She will give them hell."

"What about Martin?"

His expression turned noncommittal. "Martin is a nice guy and Briana loves him but he's not a fighter. Briana will be the one rescuing him if either of them has the opportunity. Martin will be a great husband and father for the long haul. He's the kind of guy that once he makes a decision there's no going back. He'll be faithful and true."

"But he doesn't deserve your sister," she teased.

Billie glanced at her. "No one does."

"They sound like a perfect couple." She and Alex were that way. They were different but in ways that complimented each other. They were happy.

She stared out her window and wondered if she would ever find that kind of happiness again. Not once in three years had she even thought such a thing.

Her eyes darted in the direction of Billie. He prompted those thoughts. Or maybe she'd have to take moments of happiness and be satisfied with those.

By the time the digital clock on the dash flicked to one p.m., Charly figured those guys weren't coming out—at least from this side of the property.

"It's time we have a look around back," Billie suggested, clearly thinking the same thing. He started the SUV and nosed up to the road.

"Take a right."

They drove for three miles and she instructed him to take the next left. In another two miles they reached the road she'd told him about. "Go left here, too."

He made the turn.

"There's a narrow little turn off on the left..." She leaned forward. "It's not marked because it doesn't really go anywhere. We're almost there...turn there."

He made the left and they drove about a quarter mile into the woods before the narrow dirt road ended. There was a double gate but no road beyond it. Just a path. Wide enough for UTVs.

"Now we walk," she told him.

He shut off the engine. "Do you have any idea where that cabin is located?"

"I do." She laughed. "I hid in the hatchback of Kerrick's first vehicle when he picked up my sister once. They came to party here. It was the only time she ever agreed to a date with him."

"You rode all the way here." He frowned then. "How'd you get home?"

"I took a guy's cell phone and called my dad."

Confusion dominated his expression. "You did what?"

"The guy was passed out on the ground. I slipped his phone out of his back pocket and made the call. Then I walked back out to the road and waited for him."

"What did your father say about this?"

"He wasn't happy, but he was far more interested in how these kids were getting alcohol and whatever else they were partying with. He sent a couple of deputies to check things out. Half my sister's class was grounded for weeks."

Billie laughed. "Did your sister ever find out it was you?"

"No way! It was my secret. Mine and my dad's."

"Have you been back here since then?"

She shook her head. "But don't worry. I can find it."

"As you say—" he opened his door "—famous last words."

She waved him off. It might take some time, but she would find it.

And whatever Kerrick and his pals might be keeping there.

Chapter Fourteen

3:00 p.m.

So it took her two hours.

Since there were no indications anyone had come in from the direction she and Billie did, she had no choice but to sweep from one direction to the other before moving forward in a sort of zigzag. If there had been a trail before, it was long overgrown now. This way of moving forward was slow going but it was also the best effort to ensure they didn't miss anything. Particularly since Billie had asked her to help him look for indications someone had accessed the cabin from this direction.

The downside was that they had found nothing so far.

She stalled, surveyed the spot to her right again. She smiled.

Maybe she had just gotten lucky. A couple of thin little broken limbs on a scraggly bush suggested someone or something—maybe a deer—had brushed too close. She looked for signs of deer droppings, found none. Drawing in her zigzag pattern more tightly, she quickly found another indication of foot travel. Trampled-down greenery, the lower wild grasses and a fern.

She crouched down for a closer inspection. The partial impression of a footprint was just barely visible. She waved Billie over and pointed to her find. When Billie crouched to join her, she indicated the immediate area around them. She explained, keeping her voice down to a near whisper, "I'm not seeing more so I'm thinking this is where someone who had tripped caught themselves, forcing more pressure onto this one foot. It didn't happen recently…maybe yesterday. The plants are starting to spring up again."

He studied the area a moment then nodded. "You're right. They picked their way carefully through here, then for some reason stumbled." He spoke quietly as well. "They were moving toward the road."

Charly studied the impression more closely. "I think whoever it was, he or she was barefoot." She pointed to a small, slightly deeper impression. "That looks like a big toe."

"You're right. Someone was maybe trying to get away from something or someone."

His words sent a shiver down her spine.

With this find, they had to assume someone had been here recently and that someone could still be nearby. Unless they had made it to the road.

Charly stood, placed her own hiking boot alongside the impression. Billie watched. When his gaze met hers, she said, "Too small for a man."

He pushed to his feet, stood beside her and surveyed the dense woods. "Had to be a woman or a kid."

Though her heart kicked into a faster rhythm, Charly knew better than to get too excited with nothing more than a single partial footprint. "Let's keep going forward. I'll focus on this tighter area."

"I'll take the outer perimeter."

Watching her every step, Charly moved back into that zigzag pattern. She studied the bushes…the saplings…the ground. It was slow going but that was the only way to avoid missing anything. She might still overlook a broken twig or trampled weed, but she would do her best not to miss a thing.

The cell phone in her back pocket vibrated. She groaned softly and tugged it out. Could be Shelly with a registration problem.

She frowned. *Billie.* She answered the call, surveying the area around her until she spotted him. He was a few yards ahead, to the right of her position.

"Yeah?" Again, she spoke softly.

"Obvious signs of movement here."

A spike of anticipation hit her veins. "You want me to come there or keep moving this way?"

"I'll follow this trail. You keep looking where you are."

She nodded and ended the call, tucked the phone back into her pocket. Moving as quickly as she dared without compromising her search, she worked her pattern. On her far left, north of the previous find, she discovered a new path. Compressed weeds and grasses, broken limbs…this was more than someone moving through the area. This was a struggle. At least one more distinct impression along with the previous one. This one larger, definitely a shoe or boot but not full impressions. The ground just wasn't soft enough. Plus, the grasses and decaying leaves prevented full contact with the soil in any given area.

She started to call Billie but then she spotted it…the cabin.

More of that adrenaline flowed inside her. She snapped a pic and sent it to him, then followed the tracks. One person, she decided. There were two at the place where the struggle happened, but only one from there headed to the cabin. Did that mean the person with the larger feet had overtaken the smaller person and then carried them to the cabin or maybe back to the cabin? Her phone vibrated and she checked the screen. A pic from Billie was a selfie showing him standing at the cabin door. Charly laughed to herself.

She made it the rest of the way to the cabin. She felt breathless with anticipation, hope. The cabin was old, not maintained. Moss had pretty much covered the roof. Vines had grown over the siding, obscuring the only window on the side she approached. She rounded a corner. No Billie, just more viney overgrowth and a single window. She stopped at the window and peered inside, but it was blocked by something. She couldn't say if it was some sort of curtain or what, but it obscured all beyond it.

Billie stood at the door. Yeah. She remembered that door. Though she hadn't gone into the cabin that one time she was here. Groups of kids had been all around the clearing—not much of a clearing now. The place was all grown up. Back then, when she was fourteen, there had been campfires going and kids drinking and dancing. Music playing. The remembered sounds whispered through her.

"Did you look inside?" she asked as she approached Billie.

He surveyed the area, his tension palpable. "I was waiting for you."

Rather than respond, she grabbed the knob and gave

it a twist. Didn't budge. She tried twice and had no luck. "It's locked." She banged on the door. "Hello! Anyone in there?"

Silence inside and around them seemed to close in. Disappointment wrapped around her skull and compressed. She wanted to find his sister and her husband. She didn't want the worst to be the way this ended. There had to be something somewhere! Someone who had seen or heard something! Damn it!

"I checked the other end." He nodded to the side opposite of where she had come around the house. "There's a window but like all the rest, it's covered from the inside."

She made up her mind then and there. "We have to get this door open."

He held her gaze a moment. "We're already trespassing. Do you want to add breaking and entering as well?"

"I do." She slammed her shoulder into the door to prove her point. It didn't budge. She grimaced, rubbed her arm. Definitely not as easy as it looked in the movies.

"Give me a sec," he said. He withdrew something from his pocket and crouched next to the door.

She surveyed the woods, looking for any movement, before setting her attention back on him. It was a typical generic locking knob. Shouldn't be that difficult—as if she knew one thing about picking a lock. She knew nothing about getting a lock undone other than with a key.

The door suddenly swung inward.

Charly grinned. "Oh that was good, Mr. Jagger."

"If you have no qualms about breaking and entering," he reminded her.

"Never done it until now. It's kind of cool."

"But illegal."

"Wait." She frowned. "Didn't we hear a noise? Like a cry for help. Doesn't that suggest exigent circumstances?"

He laughed; a short, dry sound. "You have watched too many movies."

"Yeah, guess I have."

They held each other's gaze and then peered into the cabin. Beyond where they stood, the interior was completely dark with just a slice of gray from the part of the door opening their bodies didn't block. The little jovial exchange had been more about not wanting to go inside. If they did and found nothing…or found something really bad…

As if he'd read her mind, their gazes locked again. "In this situation we'll ignore the usual decorum and I'll go first."

Charly gestured to the open door. "Be my guest."

As he entered, she held her breath. Though he had turned on the flashlight from his phone and was aiming it inside, she couldn't slow the pounding in her chest. *Please don't let there be bodies.*

"Clear."

The word vibrated through her as she stepped inside. Hot. Stuffy. She pulled out her phone and lit up her flashlight as well. There was a rusty metal cot with an old dusty mattress atop it. A ragged quilt and pillow were tossed to one end.

The floor was cleaner than she'd expected. A little dusty but not much else. No other furniture. No nothing… Her gaze stalled. Water bottles. Empty water bottles. She forced herself to breathe.

While Billie inspected every square inch of the place,

she assessed the wood walls, looking for anything written there. No words scrawled in blood or written with anything else. Nothing hanging anywhere. The windows were covered with plywood. Whoever did it must have painted the side facing the windows black since it had been unidentifiable from that angle. What the hell were they using this cabin for?

The clink of metal had her turning back to the cot. Billie was crouched next to the cot, inspecting something there. She moved closer before she recognized what he'd found. Handcuffs…no…shackles. Attached to the cot. Her gasp drew his gaze toward her.

"The cot is secured to the floor so there was no moving it in an attempt to get away."

Then she saw the other thing he held…shiny…so thin…a necklace.

"Is that…?" She directed her light fully on his hand.

He stood up. "This is my sister's. Our grandmother gave it to her when she was thirteen. She wears it every day—even wore it on her wedding day."

A single white pearl hung on the delicate silver chain.

Goose bumps crawled over Charly's skin. "They were here." Her words were nothing more than a whisper…a thought spoken.

Billie nodded. "We should call the sheriff now."

"I think that's a damned good idea," a voice growled.

Charly whirled to find Kerrick Rogers glaring at them from the open door.

Charly had never been afraid of anyone—Alex had said it was her one weakness. But right now, with Kerrick holding a rifle aimed in their direction, she was very definitely scared.

"We've been looking for you," Billie said calmly as if he'd been expecting the man.

Kerrick glowered at him. "Call him," he said to Charly, averting his eyes from the beam of her phone's flashlight. "Call Malone."

"We can talk about this outside," Charly offered as she lowered the beam to his chest, or more specifically, to the rifle. "Or at your house."

Kerrick's head moved firmly side to side. "We're all staying put until Malone gets here."

"Make the call," Billie said to her. "We're not the ones who have something to hide."

"What the hell does that mean?" The barrel of the weapon shifted fully on Billie.

Charly ignored Kerrick's response and did what Billie said. She tapped the number. Sheriff Malone was in her contacts. Had been for years.

"It means exactly what it sounds like," Billie said without answering the question.

The sheriff answered and Charly turned away from the other conversation to give him a quick overview of the situation, including the fact that Kerrick was armed. Behind her she could hear the low rumble of Billie's voice as well as the more threatening tone of Kerrick's.

She ended the call as quickly as she could and shifted back to the situation growing increasingly tense.

"I don't know what the hell you two are doing here," Kerrick warned, "but moves like this could get you killed. I could have shot you."

Charly cleared her throat. "Sheriff Malone is on his way. Let's just cool down and let him handle this."

"Fine by me." Kerrick leaned against the door frame but kept his rifle aimed on Billie.

Charly drew in a sharp breath and moved closer to him. She was not allowing anything to happen to him. No way.

Marshall County Sheriff's Department
Blount Avenue, 6:00 p.m.

"IT WAS MY IDEA," Charly insisted for about the twentieth time.

Tully Malone leaned back in the chair behind his desk, his hands resting against his flat stomach, fingers interlocked. "I'm sure you're well aware of the laws regarding trespassing and breaking and entering, Charly. Your daddy was a sheriff for how many years?"

"I swear," she argued. No way in hell was he putting this on Billie. She had to make him understand this one was on her. "How do you think he even knew about that cabin? I took him there and suggested we have a look."

Damn it. Sheriff Malone had separated them as soon as he and two of his deputies arrived. Sent Billie in the cruiser with the deputies while she was escorted to his vehicle. Once they arrived here they had been put in different rooms. Billie in an interview room and her in the sheriff's office. Kerrick had been allowed to follow in his own vehicle and was God knows where.

"He says he found it via a special search app his agency has available." The sheriff leaned forward, his forearms coming to rest on his desk. "That's the thing about PIs, Charly. They don't play by the rules. Now he's dragged you into this and I know this isn't your doing."

She held up her hands. “How many times do we have to go over this? It was me.”

“You’ve never had any trouble with the law before,” he argued. “Why would you suddenly start now?”

She blew out an exaggerated breath. “Whatever you choose to believe, but I’m telling you I showed him where that cabin was. It took me over two hours to find it. But that’s irrelevant. What matters is that there are shackles and a cot in that cabin. More important, there was a necklace belonging to Briana Willard. That, Sheriff Malone, is what you should be looking into. What you’re doing—” she glared at him more fiercely as she said the next part “—is wasting time.”

He heaved a big breath—almost as overblown as the one she’d expelled. “You, of all people, should know these things take time. And it doesn’t help when folks start causing a stir that I have to stop my important investigative work to look into.”

“Really?” she demanded.

He held up his hands in surrender. “The PI is trying to locate a photo of his sister wearing that necklace so we can confirm his allegation. Meanwhile, I’ll be interrogating Kerrick next. Right now—no matter how much you want to believe I don’t know how to do my job—I’m letting him stew. I confiscated his rifle because it was clear to me he’d been smoking weed.”

“Well, thanks for that,” she said, not sounding all that thankful. Her heart wouldn’t stop pounding because she knew. She absolutely knew that Kerrick Rogers had something to do with Briana’s and Martin’s disappearances. Not to mention Billie had no reason to lie about the necklace. The whole confirmation thing was just another waste of time.

As a matter of fact, sitting here debating the possibility was a waste of time!

"Charly," he said with a pointed look at her, "you need to step back and let us do our job."

"Fine." She pushed to her feet. "Then let us go home and get on with it."

He stared at her for a moment. "Deputy Lathan will take you home. I still have some questions for Mr. Jagger. He'll be here awhile longer."

And then it will be dark and there will be no more searching. For one moment she almost decided to stay. But there were things she could do before dark if she left now.

"Fine. I want to go home. Now."

He seemed surprised at her turnaround. She didn't care as long as she was out of here and could do what she needed.

"Hang on a minute." He stood, walked around his desk and out the door, closing it behind him.

Less than a minute later Cohen Lathan showed up, opened the door and poked his head in. "Let's go, Charly."

She rolled her eyes as she walked out to join him in the corridor. Couldn't her ride have been provided by anyone else?

He put a hand to her back and guided her to an exit. When they reached the parking lot, he opened the front passenger's-side door of his cruiser.

She settled into the seat and sat silently while he drove her home. He rambled on about how foolish what she and Billie had done was and that if they were lucky the Rogerses would let it go and not press charges.

She said nothing. Not one word. Not even when she got out at her cabin. He turned the vehicle around and drove away without her uttering a single syllable.

Shelly stood on the porch. "What happened?"

Charly had sent a text to let her know she would be late. "You don't want to know." She didn't have time to explain. "I need your help, Shelly. Can you stay here and see after things until I get back? It might be late. I mean really late."

She didn't like leaving the property for long when there were guests.

"Sure." The concern on her friend's face warned she had questions, but she didn't ask. Good friends didn't.

"I just have to grab a few things." Before going inside she glanced at the truck Vince had left her, thankful for the first time that he'd made the overture.

Shelly followed her into the kitchen. Charly tossed her shoulder bag onto the table, grabbed a flashlight, a bottle of water and her father's hunting rifle.

"Charly," Shelly said, her voice heavy with worry, "what're you doing?"

"When Billie gets here," she said without answering the question, "tell him I went back. He'll know what to do."

And then she left.

Chapter Fifteen

7:55 p.m.

Finding the cabin was easy this time. She basically walked straight to it. The only real problem Charly had was that it was approaching full-on dark. She had maybe thirty or forty minutes, possibly a little more, before she wouldn't be able to see without her flashlight.

She had to move fast. But first, she needed to get her bearings, so for a long moment she stood very still and considered where she was relative to the rental cabins on the Rogerses' property. She pictured north and south in her mind. The front outer boundary of the Lost in the Woods Getaway should be straight ahead of where she was standing. Of course there were acres and acres of woods between her and that front entrance. But it was all about imagining where she was with respect to everything else. Her father had taught her to do that whenever she thought she was lost. The way she had explored when she was little, she had gotten lost in their woods plenty of times.

"Here goes nothing," she muttered as she set off. The rifle was slung over her shoulder, the leather strap digging into her flesh with the weight of it. She'd tucked the bottle of water into one back pocket and her phone, set to vibrate, in the other. She held the old-fashioned Maglite flashlight in her right hand. It had been her father's. It was a damned good flashlight and heavy enough to be used as a weapon if needed. She would much prefer using it to aim the rifle at someone.

But she would do whatever necessary to protect herself.

She walked with a light step. That was something else her father had taught her. There was walking and there was stomping. Deer walked. People stomped. At least when it came to exploring the woods, he would explain. The man had been over six feet and about one hundred eighty pounds and he walked like a cat. Soundless. Purposeful.

As she traveled through the trees, skirting the thicker masses of shrubs and undergrowth, she thought of how Briana and her husband may have escaped the old cabin. Had they been caught and taken to a different location? Maybe another place on the property. Or was all the effort too late? Maybe those signs of movement around the cabin were from when they were picked up by the really bad guys. They could be far away from here by now. Or worse…dead.

What kind of person sold another human being like a piece of furniture?

She was just about to click on the flashlight when she heard a voice. She stopped…didn't move…didn't even breathe.

A light came on in the near distance.

Cabin.

Charly must have reached the edge of the Getaway area. Like the cabins at her place, these were scattered at good distances apart to provide greater privacy. She estimated the one she was approaching sat the farthest from the property entrance and business office.

"Just calm down."

Male.

Not a voice Charly recognized, at least not from this distance. That he'd growled the words didn't help, either.

If she was going to identify the person speaking, she needed to be closer. Slowly...carefully...she eased in the direction of the light. She paused just long enough to shift the Maglite so that she was holding it like a hammer ready to swing.

Another voice shattered the silence. "You don't understand. He may say the wrong thing if we don't intervene."

Female. Shrill.

The woman speaking was upset, and Charly recognized her identity as well as why she was upset.

Laney Rogers was distraught that her son was being questioned by the sheriff. Was the man whose voice Charly heard the woman's husband, Kerwin?

Charly moved closer. She needed to hear what they were saying. Surely, Laney and her husband had no idea what their son was doing...but Charly couldn't be certain. No, she decided, that couldn't be right. Laney was condescending and sometimes rude but she wasn't...

"The single problem we have is the necklace," the man said.

Not the husband.

Charly went cold...ice-cold. She recognized the voice. Laney said something else but the words were lost to Charly's utter denial.

No. That couldn't be right. She had to have heard wrong.

She needed to hear him again. She needed to hear better.

A few more steps and she would be right next to that window. She would be able to hear far better. The windows in these older cabins were single pane. Everything could be heard through them if standing fairly close.

Charly's chest felt tight as she eased in nearer to the structure.

"What are you doing?" Laney demanded.

Charly listened intently to see what the man would say next. Was he calling someone?

"Charly."

She swung around, her heart in her throat. Flashlight raised.

Even in the darkness she could see the barrel of his handgun. Maybe the dim light from the window made it more visible…made it all the more eerie. But the sight of it was not as startling to her as the man's identity.

"Charly. Charly. Charly. What am I going to do with you?"

She had been wrong. So so wrong.

How could a man she had known and trusted…one whose shoulder she had cried on…whom she had adored like an uncle be involved in this?

She fought back the shock and squared her shoulders. "Hello, Paul."

Marshall County Sheriff's Department
Blount Avenue, 8:45 p.m.

BILLIE HADN'T CALLED one of the agency attorneys. He had known the sheriff would have to release him sooner rather than later. He had nothing to hold Billie on unless trespassing or breaking and entering was being charged. Since that hadn't happened, it was only a matter of time before he could walk.

The door opened once more and Billie waited while the sheriff made himself comfortable on the other side of the table. "Cohen tells me," Malone said, "that you're sticking to your story about knowingly trespassing and breaking and entering."

"I wouldn't think of telling you anything less than the truth." Billie held his gaze until the other man flinched.

"Well, you proved the necklace—or at least one like it—belonged to your sister. Considering it would be a pretty big coincidence if it belonged to someone else and we've established that you don't believe in coincidences, I'm giving you the benefit of the doubt here and assuming the necklace you found belonged to Briana Willard."

"Belongs," Billie corrected. Malone looked confused. "*Belonged* is past tense. My sister is alive. We just have to find her before it's too late."

"If we're lucky," Malone agreed. "To that end, I'm holding Kerrick Rogers overnight. See if he'll give us anything."

"Did he call an attorney?" A smart man would. Billie hoped he wasn't that smart.

Malone shrugged. "He would if I let him but I'm not."

Billie laughed, couldn't help himself. "You're telling me you're ignoring his legal right to counsel?"

"Nope." Malone shook his head. "I just didn't give him the chance to ask for one." His gaze narrowed. "I've been doing this job a long time, Mr. Jagger. I can read people pretty good. Kerrick has something to tell me.

He just hasn't worked up the courage to do it yet. I'm giving him time to get right with himself without outside interference."

Billie gave him a nod. "I'm sure you are aware that you can't pull a tactic like that on me."

"I'm aware all right." He stretched his neck, right then left. "This is what I think, Mr. Hotshot PI. Kerrick has gotten himself involved with some bad people and he's acting as a scout—I think they call them in the business."

They might not be on the same page but they were certainly in the same chapter, so Billie waited for him to go on.

"I can't be sure, of course. Maybe one of his friends dragged him into it. I don't know that part yet but we're rounding up Perry Hillard and Finn Grayson. We'll put a little fear in them, see what they spill."

"Does that mean I'm free to go?" Billie asked, weary of the waiting game.

"That's what I came to tell you." Malone pushed back his chair. "You are free to go. Your SUV is waiting outside. If we have more questions or if the Rogers family wants to pursue any sort of charges, I'll be in touch."

Billie had a feeling the Rogers family had no idea about any of this just yet. Not that he minded. He stood and followed the man from the room. In the corridor he asked, "Where's Charly?"

Malone mulled over the question a moment. "Oh yeah. Deputy Lathan took her home just after seven."

Worry nagged at Billie. "Thanks."

He strode out of the station and hurried to his SUV. If Charly had been taken directly home, Billie didn't trust her not to go off on her own. As he drove away, he called her cell.

Three rings and then voice mail.

“Damn it.”

He drove faster.

It took what felt like a lifetime to reach Deep Woods Trail. He made the turn and pulled up to her cabin, parked next to an SUV he recognized as belonging to Shelly… the assistant that helped Charly out from time to time.

He exited the vehicle, scanning the area around him for any sign of trouble. Whatever else had happened tonight, at least some of the players Billie was convinced were involved in Briana’s and Martin’s abductions had been given a wakeup call. They now knew with a full measure of certainty that he was here, and he intended to take them down just as soon as he found his sister and her husband.

But he did not want Charly to pay the price for his moves. He’d already allowed her to grow far too deeply involved, putting her directly in the line of fire.

He knocked on the door. Waited for her to answer, but when the door opened it was Shelly. Judging by the look on her face, she was in serious distress.

“Where’s Charly?” he asked as he stepped inside.

“I don’t know. She left just before eight. I tried to talk her out of it, but she wouldn’t listen.” Her hands wrung together in front of her. “I haven’t heard back from her in all this time, and I’ve called her cell and it just goes to voice mail.”

His concern moved to the next level. “Tell me exactly what she did when she got here.”

Shelly took a breath. “She asked me to stay until she

got back. She said it might be late. Then she rounded up a flashlight, a bottle of water…" Her face scrunched as if she could barely hold back the tears. "She took her father's hunting rifle."

His jaw clenched to hold back a wave of curses. Not good. Not good at all. "Did she say anything about where she was going?"

Shelly took another of those slow, deep breaths. "She said: 'When Billie gets here tell him I went back. He'll know what to do.'"

The concern escalating inside him turned to fear. "You're certain those were her exact words."

Shelly nodded.

He hesitated. "Did she take that white truck that was sitting out there?"

"The one Vince left, yes."

"Thanks, Shelly. Hold down the fort."

When he reached the door, her voice stopped him. "Are you going to find her and bring her home?"

He glanced back at the woman so very worried about her friend. "I am."

Not only was he going to bring Charly home, he was bringing his sister and her new husband home, too.

Lost in the Woods Getaway
Scottsboro Highway, 9:45 p.m.

BILLIE PARKED OUTSIDE the cabin that served as the office and the home to the Rogers family compound. Both the vehicles that had been here before were here now, which hopefully meant the owners were home. He'd driven the road that wound behind the property and found the white truck Vince had lent Charly but it was too damned dark and he didn't have the time to try to find her in those woods.

Instead, he'd come straight to the center of activity—to the source. From the number of guests he noticed in the glass dome in the center courtyard, a dinner party was happening. He imagined the Rogers family would not want trouble. That would work to his advantage because Billie was ready to unleash exactly that—trouble. He unlocked the glove box and reached inside. He didn't carry a weapon even when on the job unless it was absolutely necessary.

This was one of those necessary moments.

He climbed out of the SUV, tucked the weapon into his waistband at the small of his back. When he reached the door that displayed the office hours and this was well past, he banged hard. Hard enough to shake the wooden slab in its frame.

There were lights on in the cabin but not in this front room. He pressed a doorbell that hopefully sent an alarm to the living quarters to let whoever was inside know someone was at the door. He waited patiently for ten, then fifteen seconds. The lights came on in the room and he banged on the door again for good measure.

"All right, all right, I'm coming," a man called out.

The door opened and Billie was ready. He held his weapon so that it would be the first thing the man saw.

His eyes rounded and his mouth did the same. Lucky for both of them no sound came out.

"Step back," Billie ordered, "unless you want the guests having dinner over there to hear and see this."

The man shuffled back awkwardly. "We…we don't keep money here."

"I don't want your money," Billie said as he closed the door behind him. "I'm looking for Charly Nix. She's here and I need you to take me to her."

"Charly." He frowned. "Why would she be here?"

Did this man have no idea what his son was doing? Billie wasn't giving him the benefit of the doubt.

"She and I were both here earlier this afternoon," Billie said. "We had a confrontation with Kerrick. We've spent the last several hours at the sheriff's office. Kerrick is still there. They're keeping him overnight."

The man's face paled. "I have no idea what you're talking about. What's Kerrick done?"

This was taking far too much time. "The cabin back in the woods on the other side of the property."

He nodded, his gaze still tracking the muzzle of the handgun. Billie lowered his weapon to refocus the man's attention on him. Whatever was going on here, he needed this guy to pay attention and to do as he said.

"Someone was being held prisoner in that cabin. I need you to tell me who, besides your son, uses that cabin."

The idea that Kerrick had insisted on calling the sheriff still nagged at Billie but there was always the chance someone in the sheriff's department was working with him, which would explain why he had no worries in doing so. At this point Billie couldn't be sure about anything. He was working with possible scenarios and pieces of potential evidence.

The man's head was moving side to side now. "No one." Then his face changed. "Wait. No. Paul Grant uses it sometimes for hunting. He's the only person we allow to hunt the land, but he hasn't been back there recently."

Billie thought of the man who had hugged Charly when they visited him. "Do you have a UTV?"

He nodded, then shook his head. "We use golf carts. They're quieter." A ringing sound drew his attention toward the door that led to the living quarters. Cell phone. It rang a second time.

"Get the key." Billie glanced at his bare feet. "And your shoes."

"Can I answer the phone? It's probably my wife." He blinked, his eyes so large he looked like an owl. "Or it could be Kerrick, I guess."

Billie didn't bother telling him that his son wasn't getting any calls tonight. "No. Just your shoes and the key for one of the golf carts. We're in a hurry."

He followed Rogers into his living room where the older man jammed his feet into the shoes he had discarded. He glanced longingly at the phone but didn't go for it.

As they exited the home through the back door, Rogers flipped on the rear exterior lights. Two carts were lined up under a carport. As he slid into the passenger seat, Billie noted a small oil stain in the gravel a few feet away. Maybe they parked farther over sometimes or maybe they had a third cart. A third cart made sense since the wife wasn't home. She could be out there somewhere with Charly. The idea knotted in Billie's chest.

Once they were loaded up, Billie withdrew his gun again. "Take me to that cabin."

Rogers nodded.

When he shifted into gear, Billie warned, "Don't do anything stupid, Mr. Rogers."

"No. No. I won't."

When they entered the tree line, Billie noted there was a path just wide enough for the carts. "Are there paths like this all over the property?"

"Mostly in this front part of the property for the cabins," he explained, glancing nervously at Billie as he spoke. "There are a couple paths farther back but none that go right up to the cabin you're talking about. We'll have to walk part of the way."

Billie scanned the dark woods around them. His gut twisted with mounting worry. If Charly wasn't here…

Another set of headlights appeared in the distance.

"That must be my wife. There was an issue at that back rental, cabin fourteen. She went to try and resolve it." He glanced at Billie, appearing even more anxious now. "She's very good at taking care of guest issues."

"Is she alone?" Billie asked. The other cart had stopped a few feet away. The headlights preventing him from seeing the interior of the vehicle.

"Oh yeah. She's alone," Rogers assured him.

Laney popped out of the driver's side of the other cart. Billie ensured his weapon wasn't readily visible as she hurried over to the driver's side of their cart. She looked at her husband first then at Billie. "Is everything all right?"

"This man," Rogers said, "seems to think Charly is at the old cabin."

Laney blinked once, twice. "I can't imagine why."

"Did you know Kerrick is in trouble again?" Rogers asked.

Billie heard movement on his right. He whipped toward the trouble. Too late. A muzzle rested against his forehead.

"Well, now, the gang's all here. Shall we start the party?"

Paul Grant.

"Where's Charly?" Billie inquired. His fingers tight around his weapon.

"He's armed," Rogers announced.

"Of course he is," Grant said with a chuckle. He pressed the muzzle of his own weapon a little harder against Billie's forehead. "Give me your gun and we'll talk about your question."

Billie reached outward as if he intended to hand over his weapon…but there was a problem with that move. A smart man never gave up his gun…otherwise, he ended up a dead man.

His arm went up fast, slammed against Grant's while his upper body plowed into the man's midsection.

The blast of a bullet leaving the chamber of Grant's gun echoed in the darkness.

Grant hit the ground, Billie on top of him. He scrambled up, his gun still clenched in his right hand. He grabbed the bastard on the ground and yanked him up as well. He dragged him toward the other cart, the one Laney Rogers had been driving.

Screaming drew his gaze over his shoulder. Laney was attempting to staunch the flow of blood coming from her husband's shoulder. The round Grant pulled off must have nailed him.

Billie shoved Grant across the passenger seat and into

the driver's seat. "Take me to Charly or I swear to God I will shoot you right now."

While the scumbag drove, Billie's gun boring into his temple, he called Malone and warned there was a gunshot victim near cabin fourteen on the property at Lost in the Woods Getaway.

The beam of the headlights bobbed across the front of a cabin. Grant stopped the cart, shut off the engine. "She's in there."

Billie switched the gun to his other hand so he could grab Grant by the collar and drag him out of the vehicle. He didn't care if the bastard walked, crawled or was dragged…they were going in together.

They reached the steps. Billie pulled Grant up with him, then he shoved him against the door. "Open it," he ordered.

Chapter Sixteen

It was the screaming that Charly heard first.

Woman...blood curdling sound.

She tried to sit up. The gag in her mouth was too tight. She listened. She'd heard something. Screaming, she was certain of. But a popping sound before that. Gunshot, she thought.

Please don't let it be Briana.

She rocked herself to her side and tried to see through the darkness. There was something happening outside.

Paul had tied her up while Laney yelled at him about how the hell they were going to fix all this. Paul had said something about putting her with the others. Charly had a sick feeling she understood exactly what that meant.

A sound at the door had her heart stuttering.

Were they coming back?

Had they decided to kill her instead?

The door opened and someone stumbled in, hit the floor. Charly drew back against the wall. Her heart thundered.

The light came on…the brightness blinded her. She tried to force her eyes open…to see.

Paul Grant was on the floor. Blood on his face. He raised his head and stared at Charly.

"Charly!"

Her attention darted away from the man she had thought was her friend to the one at the door.

Billie.

He was here.

Tears spilled from her eyes.

He was suddenly kneeling next to her. He removed the gag. Relief flooded her.

"You okay?" he asked.

She nodded. "Martin." She cleared her throat. "Martin is in the other room. He's hurt." Her gaze locked with Billie's. "Bad, I think."

Billie's jaw hardened. "I need a knife."

He got to his feet, grabbed Paul by his collar and dragged him toward the kitchen area as if he were a rag doll. Billie opened and closed drawers until he found a knife, then he dragged Paul back to where Charly was.

"Move," he warned the man, "and you know what will happen." Then he turned to Charly. "Hold your hands up."

She did as he instructed. Careful not to get the sharp edge of the blade against her skin, he cut through her bindings. She rubbed her wrists. Relief rushed through her. "Thank you."

He did the same at her ankles where the ropes were especially tight. She stretched her feet, grateful to be free. Thank God. Thank God.

Then he handed the gun to her. "I need to check on Martin. Don't take your eyes off Grant. If he moves, shoot. Shoot until he stops."

Charly took the gun in both hands, held it tight, the business end pointed at the man who had betrayed her…

who had been ready to turn her over to human traffickers. “Gladly,” she snarled.

Paul held up a hand. “You don’t understand.”

Fury streaked through her. “Move your mouth or hand again,” she spat the words at him, “and you’ll regret it.”

Billie came back into the room, Martin leaning heavily on him. “EMS is on the way,” he told Charly. He ushered Martin into a chair.

In that single instant of stupidity that she looked away, Paul grabbed for the gun.

She pulled the trigger.

The air flew out of her lungs.

Blood bloomed on her longtime friend’s upper arm. He howled in agony.

Billie came over, pushed the gun and her hands downward since she was still holding it in a firing position. Then he knelt next to Paul and inspected the injury. “You’ll live.”

Charly managed to draw in a gasp of air. Thank God. As much as she hated the man right now for what he’d done, she didn’t want to be responsible for his death.

“Where,” Billie asked, his hand flat on the other man’s injured shoulder, slowing the flow of blood, “is my sister?”

Charly held her breath…prayed they were about to hear that she was alive and close by.

When Paul only stared at him, Billie’s fingers tightened on the man’s shoulder and the bastard cried out. “You do not want me to do what I am prepared to do to get that answer,” Billie warned.

“A shipping container.”

He rattled off the number and the address. Charly knew the place.

"If you're lying to me," Billie promised, "I will make you regret it." He loosened his grip on the injured shoulder.

Paul gasped for air. "Unless they've taken them already," he said haltingly, "she's there."

"We have to hurry," Charly said, fear throttling through her.

The door suddenly burst open. Charly instinctively turned the gun in that direction. Laney Rogers stood there, the rifle belonging to Charly in her hands. She glared at Billie. "You're a dead man."

"Shoot," Billie said under his breath as he raised his hands in surrender. "Now!" He rolled to the right.

Charly pulled the trigger.

Laney fell to the floor, issuing those bloodcurdling screams again. Charly had shot her in the calf. The rifle had flown from her hands. If she'd pulled the trigger, she hadn't pulled it hard enough because the weapon didn't fire.

Sheriff Malone and several of his deputies suddenly poured into the cabin, stepping over and around Laney.

Charly only then noticed the lights flashing outside. EMS personnel were the next to crowd into the cabin.

Then everything started to happen at once. Martin was rushed away. Paramedics were seeing to Laney and Paul.

"He killed my husband," Laney screamed.

"Kerwin is on his way to the hospital," Malone assured her. "The paramedic thinks he had a heart attack but he's stable for now. Laney Rogers, you are under arrest."

While the sheriff read Laney her rights, another deputy was doing the same with Paul even as he was loaded onto a stretcher.

Billie grabbed Charly by the arm. He tucked the gun she'd used on Laney into his belt. "We have to go now."

She nodded.

Just as they stepped off the porch, a voice stopped them.

"This part is mine," Sheriff Malone said. He came down those steps. "I have cruisers en route to the port right now. Kerwin told me where to look before I let them take him to the hospital."

"I have to be there," Billie argued.

The sheriff nodded. "You and Charly can ride with me."

Lake City Marine Transport
Lake Guntersville Park Drive, 11:42 p.m.

SHERIFF MALONE HAD the owner of the transport service on site by the time they arrived. They located the shipping container and the manager opened it. To Charly's surprise, Sheriff Malone allowed Billie to enter first. EMS was standing by.

Thirty seconds later he came out with his sister in his arms. "There are two more in there."

Billie carried Briana to the nearest ambulance, and a paramedic immediately started to examine her.

Charly's knees nearly buckled as she watched the scene play out. Deputies carried the other two women out of their prison. All were loaded into ambulances and rushed away.

Sheriff Malone ushered her and Billie back to his cruiser. "We'll follow them to the hospital."

Charly reached for the rear passenger door. "You should ride up front, Charly," he said. "We need to talk."

Billie opened the front passenger door for her and then got into the back himself.

Charly wondered if she was going to be arrested for shooting Laney. But it was either shoot or be shot.

In the backseat, Billie was speaking softly to someone on his cell phone. She figured he was letting all the parents know he'd found his sister and her husband. Charly's tears started to flow again. God, she was a mess.

When Sheriff Malone had maneuvered onto the street, he glanced at her. "After you and Billie left the office, Kerrick decided he had some things to say."

She could only imagine what that jerk had said. "Is he going to testify about what they've been doing?"

"He can't tell us a whole lot about the trafficking activities," the sheriff explained, "but he had some interesting stories about other things."

Charly braced herself. She had no clue but something about his voice told her it was a bombshell.

"The night your parents were murdered," he began, "Laney came home all shaken and acting crazy," he said. "He didn't pay much attention. But the next morning when he put his laundry in the basket—apparently Laney is a stickler about that—he noticed spots of blood on the blouse his mother had been wearing. And beneath the blouse was a gun. He doesn't know what happened to the gun, but he saw it. Touched it. It wasn't until later that day that he heard about your parents. But he figured the whole scenario was crazy. His mama couldn't be a killer. But when I asked Kerwin, he started crying and the paramedics had to get him to the hospital so I couldn't press the issue. But I will because I'm taking his reaction to mean she did it."

Charly stared at him in disbelief. "Are you saying Laney Rogers shot my parents?"

"I'm saying it's something I'll be looking into. I just thought you should know."

"I don't get it." She shook her head and faced forward. "Why would she do that?"

"I can't say, but maybe now you can finally stop blaming me."

Charly stared at the man she had often felt on some level had wanted her father out of the way. The man she worried hadn't done his job to the best of his ability when it came to finding her parents' killer. Was it possible that she and Jen might finally have closure on that nightmare?

She turned in the seat to check on Billie. "You okay?"

He nodded. "I am now. You?"

"Maybe. The jury's still out."

He smiled. She smiled back.

The best part of all this was that Briana and Martin were alive and out of the reach of the bastards who would have taken them away forever. And maybe Charly would have an answer to the question that had haunted her for sixteen years.

The bad part was that Billie would be leaving.

She turned around and collapsed into her seat. She wasn't ready for that…at all.

Chapter Seventeen

Saturday, July 11

Bradly Retreat
Deep Woods Trail, 3:30 p.m.

Charly made herself a cup of chai tea and settled into a rocker on her front porch. She couldn't remember when she'd last sat on the porch and enjoyed an afternoon. She also could not remember the last time she'd had to do her morning routine. Tuesday maybe?

A smile spread across her face. All because Billie had come into her life.

She drew in a deep, cleansing breath. She'd sent Shelly home this morning around four. The woman had refused to leave until Charly was showered and in bed.

She'd slept until noon. A call from Sheriff Malone had awakened her. Laney Rogers and Paul Grant had confessed to working with a human trafficking ring to select certain women and some men to fill orders. They watched their targets and then drugged and abducted them. Held them as necessary until the time of delivery. Laney used Kerrick to accompany her when watching the women. He'd had no idea what his mother was doing. His face was the one that would be found on cameras, not hers. Some mother she had turned out to be. Her husband had helped as needed, like the night he drove the black SUV to deliver Briana and Martin to the cabin on their property for safekeeping until the delivery date. Paul was the one who approached them with the offer nearly two decades ago and served as the contact with the buyer.

All for money. The Rogerses were always in trouble financially, it seemed. Which was also the reason Laney Rogers had murdered Charly's mom and dad. Sheriff Malone said she had confessed at four-thirty this morning.

Charly's parents had been talking about creating a retreat when he retired. Laney and her husband had started theirs two decades earlier and were struggling. Laney was convinced that she wouldn't be able to survive the competition. So she literally killed the competition.

Except Charly had done exactly what her parents had dreamed of and Laney had been far too afraid to risk going after her. Getting away with murder once was one thing. She hadn't dared attempt it twice—particularly with victims from the same family.

Charly drew in a deep breath and sipped her tea. So now she knew. She didn't feel any better, but she didn't have to keep looking back, which was a good thing.

Billie had called her at seven this morning, but she hadn't heard the call. She'd been in a deep coma, apparently. He'd said his parents and Martin's were on the way and he would be staying at the hospital. Briana would be released later today but Martin would be staying in the hospital for another day or so. Since the buyer had decided he didn't want Martin, he'd been ignored and suffered from serious dehydration.

Charly was so happy for Billie and the families.

Jen was coming home next weekend. She and Charly would have some time to absorb and analyze all this new information. To get right with it, so to speak. They planned to spend a private moment at their parents' graves.

Charly exhaled a big breath. It was all working out.

She laughed, set her tea aside. Except the part about losing Billie. That one was going to hurt bad for a long time to come.

He'd never been hers, she reminded herself.

But it had felt like they belonged together.

The sound of a vehicle rolling up the long drive drew her attention there. She still needed to get those security cameras. As soon as the black SUV came into view, her heart started to race.

It was Billie. She bit her lip to hold back a smile.

He parked next to the white borrowed truck and got out.

As he approached the porch she noticed that he still wore the same clothes he'd had on last night. He looked like hell and somehow at the same time he looked exactly like she imagined heaven would.

"Hey."

"Hey." At the top of the steps he leaned against the railing and just looked at her.

"How are Briana and Martin?" The sheriff had told her already but asking was expected.

"Good. Really good. My parents and his are here now so they're in good hands."

"Great." She managed a breath despite the pounding in her chest. "You need a shower and some sleep," she suggested. "I can go over to the treehouse cabin and get your things for you."

"Can we talk?" He nodded to the door. "Inside?"

"Sure." She got up, decided to come back out for her cup. Right now the way her hands were shaking, she didn't trust herself to pick it up.

When they were inside she turned back to him. "You want to sit?" She gestured to the couch.

He shook his head and then he moved closer to her. He pulled her into his arms. "I changed my mind. I just want to hold you."

She fought back tears. Damn it. What was with all the waterworks lately? She rested her cheek against his shoulder. "Okay."

He held her for a long time. She couldn't be sure how long…didn't care if she could stay exactly that way.

Then he drew away, held on to one of her hands and backed toward her bedroom, drawing her along with him. "I'm not going back to Chicago," he told her.

Her lips trembled. "You're not?"

He shook his head as he backed up against the foot of her bed.

"Do you mean now or are you saying ever?"

"I'll visit, but I want to be here with you." One by one, he slipped the buttons of his shirt free. "If that's okay with you."

She nodded. Couldn't possibly speak.

"You're the coolest, most incredible woman I've ever met, and I want you to be mine."

His shirt hit the floor and the ability to breathe deserted her.

"We can visit my family and friends from time to

time." He reached for the hem of her tee and lifted it up and over her head, tossed it aside.

"I can still do research and that sort of thing for the agency from right here while I'm helping you." He pulled her close, reached behind her and unfastened her bra. Somehow, he slid it free without her body losing contact with his.

"All that sound okay to you?"

"As long as you're sure." She moistened her lips, prayed her knees wouldn't give out.

"Oh, I'm sure." He lowered his head, brushed his lips across hers. "I watched my sister marry the man she loved last Friday and then almost lose him a few days later. I'm not taking that chance…on losing you."

She searched his eyes. "Just so you know, I'm agreeing to all this because I don't want to lose you, either. But what if after we get to know each other better, one of us changes our mind?"

He grinned. "Never going to happen."

"You're very confident, Mr. Jagger," she said, grinning right back at him.

"Because I know what the rest of my life looks like," he murmured between kisses.

"How do you know?" she whispered, her body starting to ache with need.

He drew back, stared at her for so long that she trembled. "Because I saw it in your eyes."

That was all she needed to hear.

* * * * *